SINGLED OUT

SINGLED OUT

SIMON BRETT

G.K. Hall & Co. • Chivers Press
Thorndike, Maine USA   Bath, Avon, England

This Large Print edition is published by G.K. Hall & Co., USA and by Chivers Press, England.

Published in 1995 in the U.S. by arrangement with Scribner, an imprint of Simon & Schuster Consumer Group, Inc.

Published in 1995 in the U.K. by arrangement with Macmillan General Books.

U.S. Hardcover   0-7838-1377-5   (Mystery Collection Edition)
U.K. Hardcover   0-7451-7888-X   (Windsor Large Print)
U.K. Softcover   0-7451-3713-X   (Paragon Large Print)

The text of this Large Print edition is unabridged.
Other aspects of the book may vary from the original edition.

Set in 16 pt. News Plantin.

Printed in the United States on permanent paper.

British Library Cataloguing in Publication Data available

Library of Congress Cataloging in Publication Data

Brett, Simon.
    Singled out / Simon Brett.
        p.   cm.
    ISBN 0-7838-1377-5 (lg. print : hc)
    1. Large type books. I. Title.
[PR6052.R4296S53   1995b]
823'.914—dc20   95-17661

To Drew and Ellen

PART ONE:
1973

ONE

The man looked suitable for her purposes. He sat at the bar, swirling melting ice in a glass of Scotch. His eyes darted about, undecided, unresolved. His suit, large checks, wide lapels, slight flare to the trousers, was smart, but seemed to say he was from out of town.

He was sensationally good-looking. Firm, spare body. Dark brown hair that lapped over the top of his collar and curled tightly in long sideburns. Blue eyes nestling in surprisingly luxuriant lashes.

Laura sat on the stool beside him. She shook back her dark hair and fixed her hazel eyes on his. 'Hi,' she said. 'My name's Carole.'

The room, in a hotel near Paddington, had been booked in advance, and Laura had targeted the bar after months of research in central London. The date too had been carefully chosen. Over the previous few months she had spent other evenings in the bar but not seen anyone suitable. The man was the first she had taken back to the hotel.

He said he was called David. Quite possibly he too was using a false name. Laura didn't care. His name was one of the many things about him that didn't interest her.

9

She established that he was from Manchester, in London for a business meeting the following morning. Laura asked no questions about the nature of his business, and he didn't volunteer it. The man seemed as keen to limit personal information as she was. The details of her life held no interest for him either.

But of course he was interested in fucking her. He was a man, after all.

Laura ordered a bottle of Scotch from Room Service and, when their glasses were charged, took control. She pushed away the low coffee table and sat beside him on the sofa.

'Cheers.'

The man raised his glass to hers. There was still a wariness in his eyes. He was not fazed by the unexpected turn his evening had taken, but remained on his guard. A long swallow of Scotch, then he asked in his flat Mancunian voice, 'What do you want from me?'

'I want you to fuck me,' Laura said.

He considered his reply for a moment, then half-smiled. 'Well, I dare say that could be arranged.' A new thought disturbed him. 'You're not expecting me to pay, are you? Because I can assure you when I want sex, I don't need to —'

She silenced him with a reassuring hand on his knee. 'I'm not expecting you to pay.'

'Just a bonus, is it? Why? It's not my birthday.'

'Just a bonus.'

For a moment he seemed about to ask more,

find out why he had been singled out for this largesse. Laura moved her hand along his thigh and, as she intended, lust dispelled his curiosity.

He leant forward to kiss her. His lips were firm, slightly salty in taste. Laura pressed hers against them, flicking her tongue chameleon-like into his mouth. He pressed closer, a hand reaching to the side of her face. It outlined the angle of her jaw, slid down the neck, landed lightly on her shoulder, feeling the brassiere strap through the Indian cotton of her dress.

Her finger described a wide, slow circle over his thighs and stomach, just avoiding the evident erection. Then her hand moved up to brush against the roughness of his chin. Their lips were still conjoined, her tongue teasing his forward to invade the privacy of her mouth. Laura's hand loosened his wide flowered tie and slipped between the buttons of the tightly cut shirt. Her fingers tangled lazily with the hairs on his chest, then expertly freed a couple of buttons.

His free hand cupped a breast, squeezed tentatively as if anticipating rebuff. Encouraged when none came, the hand slipped down to caress her buttocks, defining the line of her bikini briefs each time it passed. Though it was chilly October, Laura had decided against wearing tights. They would only have got in the way. The sweeps of his stroking hand grew longer, moving down the smooth muscles of Laura's thigh, ever nearer the hem of her skirt.

She felt herself moistening. The skin around

her nipples tightened and tingled. It was as she had hoped. Though her emotions stayed frigidly detached, her body was responding.

Laura drew away from the kiss and looked up into the beautiful blankness of his eyes. 'All right?' she asked.

'All right,' he mumbled back. 'I'll enjoy fucking you.'

Emboldened, his hand moved swiftly under her dress, homing along the inside of her thigh to the mound between her legs. Laura let out a little moan, part involuntary, part calculated, as a finger found the cleft of her through the thin silk. 'Shall we go on to the bed?' she murmured.

The man nodded and slowly rose to his feet, rendered cautious by the erection that strained against his trousers. He looked down at his empty glass.

Laura poured in more Scotch and placed it on the bedside table. She took hold of the bedclothes and, in one fluent movement, pulled back topsheet, blankets and coverlet so that they crumpled down to the floor at the end of the bed. The man stood watching.

'What turns you on most?' Laura asked. 'To undress yourself . . . have me undress you . . . what?'

'You undress me . . .' His voice was throaty with desire. 'Then undress yourself while I watch.'

Laura shrugged and gestured to the bed. The man unzipped shiny brown boots with a slight platform sole, kicked them off, removed his socks and came across to lie on the sheet. He propped himself up on pillows against the headboard.

The man said nothing, but watched closely as Laura removed his tie, undid the remaining buttons of the shirt and slipped it off. Her hands deftly freed the metal clasp of his waistband, then edged his zip undone over the bulge of flesh. She worked the trousers and briefs down his legs. As she slipped them off, Laura ran her hand lightly down the length of his erection. He let out an involuntary sigh.

'Very satisfactory,' said Laura. 'Now I undress . . . ?'

The man nodded.

Laura behaved as if she was relishing the routine she went through, teasing undone the buttons down the front of her dress. Slowly she reached round to unclasp the black brassiere, gradually allowing it to fall away from her tight-nippled breasts.

She slid two fingers inside the waistband of her bikini briefs, let them circle idly for a moment, then slowly worked the thin material downwards. All the time she could feel the man's heavy-lidded gaze, and it gave her a sense of power.

She stepped out of the briefs and stood facing him. Deliberately she rubbed her right hand over her breasts, snagging against the hardened nipples. Then she let it slide gently over the contour of her stomach to rest against the black bush between her legs. The man groaned. With a will of its own, his right hand moved up to encircle his penis. Laura's sense of power grew.

'Let me do that for you,' she said, moving forward.

She knelt on the bed beside him. He withdrew his hand and watched as hers formed a ring to massage the burning flesh. With each downward stroke she let a finger tickle against the puckered tightness of his scrotum. His breathing seemed to rise from deeper and deeper within his chest. Laura relaxed her fingers, widening their span so that now each stroke only dusted against him.

'Tighter,' the man moaned. 'Tighter.'

'No.' Laura spoke firmly, took her hands away and quickly moved her body to arch over him. His penis still raked the empty air as the buttocks clenched and unclenched. Supporting herself on one arm, she used the other hand to distend the opening of her wet vagina and lower herself down on to him. They sighed together as his full length slid into her.

His sighs re-formed into strangled words. 'Shouldn't I have a French letter on?'

The detached part of her brain registered the phrase. Where did he come from? How old did a man have to be to use the expression 'French letter' in the 1970s? But all she said was, 'Don't worry. Everything's fine.' Which was just as well, because seconds later he came spurting into her.

The man exhaled a huge sigh and lay limp as a glove puppet. Laura stayed astride him, feeling the little twitchings as his penis shrank away

14

inside her. 'Hope it was good for you too.' His mumbled words sounded unnatural, a quotation from some worthy tome on interpersonal relationships.

'It was fine for me,' Laura murmured. Not of course that she had come. Or even enjoyed it. But then that hadn't been the aim of the exercise.

Forty minutes later they fucked again. To have described it as 'making love' would have been inappropriate. The man seemed to feel no great need to repeat his performance, but after all her planning, Laura was determined. This time she manoeuvred him on top of her. He tried to control himself and extend the action, but she was in charge. A few well-organized twitches of her vaginal muscles and once again he had shot his load inside her.

'You made me come too quickly,' he grumbled as he withdrew.

Laura said nothing, but reached for the whisky bottle and recharged his glass. The man drank it down and lay still beside her in feigned sleep. After a few minutes a series of little shudders ran through his body as real sleep took over.

Laura looked at her watch. Half past eleven. She decided to wait and see. If nothing else was forthcoming, she'd get rid of him. Cautiously she moved out of the bed. Fluid trickled stickily down the inside of her legs, but she made no attempt to clean herself up. She picked up her handbag from by the sofa and checked inside. The metal curve of her automatic pistol's butt reassured her. She hoped she wouldn't need the gun, but was comforted to know it was there. Placing the hand-bag on the floor nearby, she lay back down on the bed.

It was about an hour before the man shuddered awake again. For a moment he gazed around blearily, uncertain where he was. With recollection seemed to come revulsion. He swung his legs round to sit on the side of the bed, his back to Laura.

'Have you got a cigarette?' he growled.

'No. I don't smoke.'

'Might've bloody known it. Pass the whisky.'

As she handed the bottle across, Laura let her hand linger on the man's shoulder. He made no attempt to remove it, so, while he poured another drink, she let her hand glide down his back, round the curve of the hips towards his penis.

'What are you — some kind of nymphomaniac?' he snapped, breaking free.

'No. I just thought we might do it again.'

'Well, I don't want to.' He sounded as petulant as a schoolboy.

'All right,' said Laura coolly. 'You'd better go.'

'What?'

'I said you'd better go.'

'Listen!' The man turned sharply towards her. His face, tightened up into an expression of fury, was no longer beautiful. 'I decide when I want to go — right! You're just a tart — a bloody

16

whore — and just because I've fucked you, it doesn't give you any rights over me!'

Laura's voice stayed even and unemotional. 'I'm not claiming any rights over you. I'm just saying it's time for you to get dressed and go.'

'Don't you order me around!'

His right hand leapt out as if to slap, but Laura was quick enough to move her face away. In spite of his beautiful body, the man looked ridiculous in his nakedness, trying to assert control. Laura hadn't intended to smile, but she must have done.

With a cry of 'You cow! Don't you dare laugh at me!', he suddenly had his hands round her neck. The pressure was light, but his muscles were rigid, ready to tighten, and the glint in his eye was ugly. Laura offered no resistance, but slipped back on to the bed, her right arm trailing over the side.

'All the bloody same, you women!' the man hissed. 'Either you won't let us have sex when we want it, or else you bloody force yourselves on us. Cunts, that's all you are — just bloody cunts!'

She had no alternative. When Laura's right arm moved up from beside the bed, the gun was held firmly in her hand. The man's blue eyes blinked in amazement as the end of the barrel was pressed against the middle of his forehead.

'I said,' Laura murmured quietly, 'that it was time for you to get dressed and go.'

He didn't speak as he released his hold and

moved cautiously away from the bed. He scrab-
bled on the floor for his clothes, and put them
on with clumsy speed. All the time he held Laura's
gaze, and all the time she kept the gun trained
on him. He didn't bother to put his tie on. At
the door he paused to throw back one final insult,
but thought better of it, and shuffled off into
the corridor.

Laura crossed swiftly to the door and double-
locked it. She never met the man again.

TWO

She found herself trembling after he had gone. Not just with relief, but also with shock at how she had behaved. It was exactly what she had intended to do, but that she had been able to do it with such detachment left her dazed and unnerved.

She replaced the covers on the bed and slid herself under them. Suddenly, as the tension drained from her, she felt exhausted. With surprising ease, she slipped into sleep.

The taxi dropped Laura Fisher outside her flat in Bayswater. She gave the driver a fifty-pence coin and told him to keep the change. As she extracted keys from the pocket of her coat, she checked her watch. Just time to change and grab some coffee. She hadn't had anything at the hotel. Up and showered early, checked out by seven, paying in cash and leaving no sign that she'd ever been there, except for the name in the register. 'Carole Saunders.'

She was opening the front door when a voice close up behind her said, 'Good morning, Laura.'

She pulled the door closed and took her key out of the lock before turning to face her husband.

'Good morning, Michael. Creeping up on me again, are you?'

He was still good-looking, though his jaw had lost the sharp outline it had had when they married in 1967. The single button of his wide-lapelled blazer strained a little over his stomach, and the restless blue eyes had sunk deeper into their sockets. His hair was thinning at the front. He no longer looked the Head Boy he had once been, but his voice still retained its public school arrogance.

'Not creeping up. Just driving past and saw you.' He gestured to the gleaming white Citroen DS parked opposite.

'Oh yes?' said Laura, disbelieving.

'Aren't you going to invite me in?'

'No,' she replied. 'I'm never going to risk being alone in a room with you again, Michael.'

They had coffee in the anonymous lounge of a nearby hotel. The other customers were a group of white-robed Arabs and a party of German students.

'This is bloody stupid, Laura,' Michael protested. 'I'm not a monster. I'm not going to hurt you.'

'It's my flat and I'll decide who I invite into it, thank you.'

He let out an exasperated sigh. 'How long are you intending to keep this up?'

'What do you mean?'

'Look, I'm very impressed. You've proved

you're capable of setting up on your own. You've rented a flat, you're paying for it out of your own money, you're independent — full marks. But the fact remains that there's a much nicer house in Richmond where you should be living.'

'I don't see that there's any "should" about it.'

'Laura, I think I've been very long-suffering over this. I've let you go your own way, do your own thing . . . I even let you go off and work in New Zealand for six months . . . but now any point that needed proving has been proved. You should come back. I'm still your husband, and husbands do have certain rights.'

Laura gazed at him in disbelief. 'Michael, don't you listen? Haven't you heard any of the things I've been saying over the last few years? Our marriage is over. We are going to get divorced.'

He shook his head with infuriating calm. 'There's no reason for us to get divorced. I haven't got anyone else. You haven't got anyone else.'

'How do you know?'

'I know. I keep an eye on what you're up to, Laura.'

She looked up sharply, but with a smug smile he avoided eye contact. His words had stimulated a suspicion which had been growing for some time, the suspicion that Michael was spying on her. That morning wasn't the first time he had appeared as if by accident. There had been occasions when Laura felt sure she'd glimpsed him on the street when she was out shopping, or seen a white DS flash by as she arrived at or left her office. She didn't think that she was getting paranoid.

'Michael, you must cooperate on this divorce. Admit we made a mistake. We married too young, before we'd found our own personalities.'

'I'd found mine. And I was established in my work. When we got married I was already a partner in the agency, for God's sake.'

'Yes, but I wasn't established in my work. Or in my personality. I am now, and I've changed. I'm different from the person you married, Michael.'

'That's certainly true. And don't imagine for a moment that I think it's an improvement.'

Laura looked down at her watch. 'I must get to work.'

He appeared not to have heard her. 'We should have started a family straight away . . .' he mused disconsolately. 'Then none of this nonsense would have happened.'

'By "nonsense" you mean my career, do you?'

'Not just your career. I mean this stupid situation we've got ourselves into — living apart, sniping away at each other all the time. We're both thirty, for God's sake.'

'Not quite in my case.'

'Near enough. What we should be doing at this time of our lives is bringing up a family.'

'What *I* should be doing I think you mean.'

'Hm?'

'If we had children, would it affect your life much?'

'Well, obviously.'

'Would you stop working, stop selling houses, stop wheeling and dealing on the property market . . . ?'

'No, of course I wouldn't, Laura.'

'But you'd expect me to.'

'I'd have to keep working to pay the bills, simply to —'

'I make more than you do, Michael.'

As ever, he was stung by this fact. He looked away shiftily, then changed tack, reaching forward to take her hand across the coffee table. 'The main thing — the thing that seems to get lost in all this other stuff — is that I love you, Laura.'

She gave him a wry look. 'I wonder.'

'I do.'

'I wonder if you actually know what love means. Perhaps you do love me, according to your definition of love.'

'And I want you.' His voice became thick and urgent. 'I want to make love to you.'

'But I don't want to make love to you, Michael.'

'Why not?'

'We've been through all this. Because love didn't seem to have anything to do with what we used to do in bed. It was just you taking me, an exercise in power. It was you trying to colonize my body.'

'Don't be ridiculous.' His voice was heavily dismissive. 'Is that a quotation from Germaine Greer or another of those — ?'

'No, it's what I think, Michael. You just wanted to control me — and planting a baby inside me would have been the ultimate form of control.'

'No, it's —'

'I'll have a child when *I* want to have a child.'

'Listen!' His hand closed fiercely over hers, crushing the bones together. 'I can only take so much of this!'

'Don't start that again, Michael.'

For a moment he could not contain the fury inside him, but then his grip relaxed. Laura withdrew her hand and rubbed it to restore the circulation.

'Now do you understand why I don't want to be alone in a room with you?'

He shook his head in exasperation. 'God, what can a man do with a bloody woman?'

'He can refrain from hitting her, for a start.'

'Laura, that only happened once or twice.' Catching sight of her expression, he looked away. 'And it wasn't as if I lacked provocation. You were my wife, for God's sake!'

'Yes, I *was*.'

'But, Laura —'

'Don't make a fuss about the divorce, Michael. Let it go through. Otherwise the domestic violence may have to be brought up in court.'

'It was hardly domestic violence.'

'Wasn't it?'

Once again he could not meet her eye. A little smile tugged at his sulky lips. 'Anyway, if it did come up in court, I'd love to know how you'd prove it. No witnesses, were there?'

'No.'

'So it'd just be your word against mine, wouldn't it, Laura?'

'Yes.'

'And most judges are men, aren't they?' said Michael smugly.

Her husband drove off in a disgruntled squeal of tyres, and Laura let herself into the house. It was a tall white building fronted by an impressive portico and black railings. Her flat was on the second floor with a view over the trees of the central square. Rented. Soon she wanted to buy her own place, but needed a few more years of high earnings. Building societies were still wary of giving mortgages to single women.

She switched on the transistor radio, which was tuned to the new commercial station, Capital, and looked round the living room. Her own space was very precious. It gave Laura enormous and continuing satisfaction to know that every item in the room was hers alone. She had chosen them, she had paid for them, they expressed her identity.

She put on the kettle in the kitchenette and, while it was boiling, changed her clothes. Basic, functional underwear, tights. Ribbed T-shirt with a row of buttons at the neck, Indian cotton dungarees. Green shoes with platform soles and appliquéd leather flowers. It was hot in the office. Better to dress as for the summer and ward off the October chill with her coat when she went outside.

She put all her dirty clothes in the washing machine. They didn't make a full load, but Laura needed to start the wash straight away. The clothes didn't exactly feel soiled, but the events of the night before required a symbolic cleansing. The unimportant details of what had happened needed to be purged away.

She ground coffee, put it into the glass funnel of the Cona and poured over hot water from the kettle; it started to percolate through. Capital Radio announced the nine o'clock news. She must hurry. The lead item was once again the fighting between Egypt and Israel in the Sinai Desert. The oil states threatened to raise prices in protest against America's support for Israel. A woman had been found strangled in a West London car park. England's football team had only achieved a 1–1 draw with Poland and wouldn't qualify for the World Cup.

Laura perched on the back of an armchair as she sipped her coffee. Facing her on the mantelpiece was a small wooden-framed mirror and beside it the photograph of her mother. As she often did, Laura shifted position so that her face filled the mirror. She and her mother matched. The hair styles were different, but the features uncannily alike. The same dark hair, the same light hazel, almost honey-coloured eyes. Everyone had always said she was the spitting image of her mother.

But Laura was determined that any parallels between them would stop at their physical likeness. In every other particular, Laura Fisher's life was going to be totally different from her mother's. She was not going to trap herself in stifling suburbia. She was not going to tamp down her emotions into acquiescent passivity. She was not going to hide unpalatable truths behind a facade of middle-class conformity. She was going to rise above her background and, by sheer willpower, make her own destiny.

Above all, Laura Fisher was determined that her life, unlike her mother's, would not be prematurely ended by murder.

THREE

'**God, am I** relieved to see you.' Rob's voice swooped in self-parodying campness as Laura entered the *Newsviews* office.

She looked at her watch. Bloody Michael's appearance hadn't made her late, had it? But no, she was all right. 'I'm on time, Rob.'

'Not what I meant, lovey.' His hand gestured languidly towards the day's bulletin board.

Amidst the usual pinned-on cuttings and notes about potential stories was a black and white photograph. It was grainy, passport-size blown up, and showed a young woman with dark hair and pale eyes.

'For a moment thought it was you, sweetie,' Rob cooed.

'Doesn't look anything like me, does it?'

'Oh yes, dear, very like.'

'I can't see it.'

'No, well, we never can, can we? We all have this image of ourselves that's totally different from what the world sees. Source of most of the tragedies that ever happen, that fact, you know, Laura dear.'

'Is it?' She grinned as she moved across to the coffee machine and filled herself a white plastic cup. As ever, it was almost too hot to hold.

She took a scalding sip.

'Oh yes,' Rob went on. 'I mean, for example, I just think of myself as an ordinary-looking workaday sort of chap . . .' He smiled in apologetic mock-naivety, '. . . but you wouldn't believe the number of men out there who think I'm just *devastating* — *gorgeous*. I don't pretend to understand it, but they just can't seem to get enough of my body.'

He sighed, perplexed by the intractable oddity of human nature.

'Do I gather from this that you had a good evening?'

'Oh, my *dear*.' He coyly fluttered his long eyelashes. 'Did I just? A good evening? I tell you, if there were Fucking Olympics, I could do it for England.'

'Good for you.'

'Mm, very good for me, thank you.' A modest little smile. 'And, I'm fairly confident, not bad for the others involved. You?'

'Me?' Laura was annoyed to find herself colouring.

'Your evening.' Rob turned an incisive stare on her. 'Did your evening turn out all right?'

She responded with a light 'Uhuh'.

'Good . . . Good . . .' He held her gaze and Laura was the one who turned away. There were times when she wished Rob didn't know her so well.

'So what were you up to, Laura? Skulking round in a false identity, on the look-out for a bit of rough trade . . . ?' She refused to be drawn, just smiled at him enigmatically. 'Hm. Certainly what *I* was doing.'

He reached out, took her hand and planted a slobbery kiss on it. Like all his actions, it was heightened, as if the gesture were being sent up. 'Anyway, glad to see you're all right.'

'What do you mean?'

'No, really got a *frisson* when that photo came in.' He nodded towards the bulletin board. 'Thought for a horrid moment it *was* you.'

Laura moved across to look more closely at the girl's face. 'Why, who is it?'

'Melanie Harris.'

A shrug. The name meant nothing.

'Girl who was found last night strangled in a car park in Paddington,' said Rob.

The Conference Room was stale with the previous day's smoke and beginning to fill with that morning's exhalations. The table presented its customary chaos of newspapers, clipboards, spiral-bound notepads and coffee cups, some scrunched up, others garnished with floating cigarette butts.

The *Newsviews* production team liked, even nurtured, scruffiness, as if it reinforced their serious journalistic credentials, gave *gravitas* to what some might regard as a lightweight programme. This attitude came from the editor, Dennis Parker, who, though he'd moved some years before to the lucrative pastures of television, allowed no one to forget his gritty Fleet Street background.

He sat at the head of the table, jacket over the back of his chair, shirt sleeves unnecessarily held up by elasticated metal bands. A broad, garishly bright tie was loosened at the neck and curved over a large stomach, legacy of the hard lunching which Dennis Parker thought essential to his image. His face had the pumice-stone surface of a heavy smoker.

The producers, directors and researchers lolled around the table with studied casualness, as if self-consciously re-creating television's image of a journalists' meeting.

Dennis's secretary sat a little behind her boss, shorthand notebook and pencil at the ready, cigarette slotted into the corner of her mouth. Laura was the only other woman in the room; she and Rob were the only people not smoking.

'I don't think we can do anything on this strangling,' said Dennis Parker definitively.

'I think we should,' Laura countered.

He looked at her through narrowed eyes. He did not like having his judgement questioned, least of all by a woman. But he gave a conciliatory smile and said, 'Listen, love. We're not in the hard news business. *Newsviews* is a news magazine programme. We're trying to make inroads into the *Nationwide* audience, not the *Panorama* one.'

'I still think we can do features on more serious subjects when they come up.'

'We are doing features on more serious subjects, love.' Each time he used the endearment he managed to make it more diminishing. 'Today we're doing this report on alternative fuels that can be used if the oil really does dry up.'

'But we're also doing the feature on how often fire brigades get called out to rescue cats caught up trees.'

'Sure. We mix the serious with the more light-hearted. That's what magazines are about, what the audience wants. Come on, that's why you read your *Women's Weekly*, isn't it, Laura?'

This got the intended ripple of masculine laughter. Laura restrained her anger and continued in a level voice, 'I still think we can use this murder as a peg for something on violence against women.'

'Oh, come on. *Newsviews* is a news magazine, not a soapbox. We aren't the bloody *Guardian* women's page. We do women's stories, yes — like that one a couple of weeks back about the girl who'd set up her own mail-order trouser-suit business — but we don't do Women's Lib stuff.'

'I'm not talking about Women's Lib, Dennis, I'm talking about crime. We always get good audience reaction when we do crime features.'

'Well . . .'

Laura took advantage of the editor's brief moment of uncertainty. 'That report I did on how easy it is to buy an illegal firearm in London got some of the best audience reaction we've ever had.'

'Yes, maybe, but —'

'And if we did a feature on the reasons why

women are the target of so much violence . . . you know, get in a psychiatrist, round up some women who've been victims of —'

'No, Laura.'

'But, Dennis —'

'I said "No". I'm editor of this programme and I'm the one who knows what fits into the *Newsviews* brief.'

'Yes, but I think you should be open to the possibility that the *Newsviews* brief can be widened.'

'Laura!'

This time she'd got him angry. He'd interpreted her words as a direct criticism of his judgement. There was no point in pursuing the argument; it would only make matters worse.

Dennis Parker sank back into his chair with some satisfaction at her silence, and continued, 'Now didn't somebody say they'd picked up a story about make-up for men . . . ?'

There was a general giggle as a young researcher moved eagerly into the spotlight. 'Yes. Found an American magazine article which said in ten years' time men'll think as little of wearing make-up in the street as women do.'

The editor chuckled. 'The day you find me wearing the stuff, you have my full permission to have me certified.'

Allowing time for the sycophantic laugh to subside, the young researcher went on, 'The article says it's a natural progression. Ten years ago a lot of men couldn't envisage wearing aftershave or deodorant . . . or washing their hair more than once a week.'

'I still think that's a bit iffy,' said the editor, who habitually went round in an aura of what he regarded as a 'natural, masculine' smell. 'All right for the pinkos and the perverts, but . . .'

A visionary look came into his eye. 'Hm. I've had a thought . . .' This was one of Dennis Parker's catch-phrases. The meeting was appropriately silent, awaiting the revelation of their editor's latest brainwave. 'We should do some *vox pops* on the idea of men wearing make-up . . . that'd be good, yes. Ask people in the street . . . women, men, try and get the odd coon . . . usual mix. Right, who'd better set that one up . . . ?'

He scanned the table, enjoying his power of allocating work. The researcher who'd brought up the idea looked almost pathetically hungry to be given the job. Dennis Parker's eyes lingered on the young man for a long, tantalizing moment, before moving on.

'You by any chance know anything about make-up for men, Rob?' The editor spoke with a hint of a lisp, and his audience provided predictable sniggers at the innuendo.

As ever, Rob played up to expectations. 'Well, maybe the teensiest bijou bitette,' he confided with a lowering of his eyelashes.

The meeting guffawed its appreciation of this sally.

'Good,' said Dennis. 'You'd better research it

then.' Ignoring the disappointment in the other researcher's face, he looked round the table. 'And who shall we delegate to direct the *vox pops* . . . ?' His eyes came to rest. 'Think this could be a good one for you, Laura.'

'The bastard!' she muttered as they walked back to the office.

'Oh, come on, lovey, don't get so heavy about it,' said Rob. 'You ought to know by now . . . Suggest an idea Dennis doesn't care for and you get rapped over the knuckles. "All right, Laura, for that you're going to have to stand in the corner with a dunce's hat on" — or go out and do some dreary *vox pops,* which comes to the same thing.'

'But it *is* a good idea — it really is.'

'Never said it was a bad idea, just said it was one Dennis doesn't care for.'

'Hm. He'd like to get me off the programme, you know.'

'I'm sure he would. But he's not going to. Dennis may be a pompous old fart, but he's not stupid. He knows you bring more original ideas to *Newsviews* than the rest of the team put together.'

Laura didn't appear comforted by this, so Rob went on, 'What'll happen is what usually happens. In a couple of weeks' time, dear Dennis will suddenly bring an editorial meeting to a standstill.' He slipped into a camp parody of the editor's fruity tones. ' "I've just had a thought . . . We ought to do something on *Newsviews* about vio-

35

lence towards women." And we'll all clap our little hands and say, "Gosh, what a brilliant wheeze! Aren't we lucky to have such a creative editor to work for!"

'Laura, the only thing you have to remember with Dennis is — wherever an idea originally came from, we've all got to pretend it's his. Allow him that little indulgence and he's an absolute pussy-cat.'

'It's so ridiculous, though, isn't it — that we have to go through that kind of pantomime?'

Rob shrugged. 'Worse things happen.'

'God, and the way he patronizes me.'

The researcher flicked his eyes heavenwards. 'You think you've got problems.'

'Yes, why do you put up with them all sniggering at you, Rob?'

'My dear, when you've been a screaming queen as long as I have, you hardly notice the sniggering any more.'

He swanned through the door into the *Newsviews* offices. 'Any messages, Esther my love?'

The senior production secretary looked up from her desk. 'Nothing for you, Rob.'

'Huh. "Nobody loves a fairy when she's forty." ' He flounced off to his desk. But through the self-parody, Laura got the feeling that Rob had been expecting a message and was hurt not to have received it.

'Couple for you, though, Laura,' said Esther. 'Oh?'

'Somebody from . . . TV Training Company,

something like that . . . asked if you'd be interested in tutoring a course on producing magazine programmes . . . ?'

'No, thanks.'

'What — don't think you'd be up to it?' Rob called across waspishly.

'No. Just don't want to. My career's still moving. Only people who're totally washed up and finished end up teaching.'

'Ooh, what a tongue you've got on you! You can be so cruel sometimes,' sighed Rob, wiping an imagined tear from the corner of his eye.

'Other message was from your brother.'

Laura turned slowly to face Esther. 'What?'

'Kent. He *said* he was your brother.'

'Yes. Yes, my brother's name is Kent.'

'He said he'd meet you here at seven after the show comes off the air.'

'I'm not sure that that'd be . . . Was there a number I could call him back on?'

'No, he was going to be out all day.'

'Oh.'

'Why? It's not a problem, is it?'

'What? No, not a problem.'

But it was. There was something uncomfortable about the idea of Kent coming to her workplace. He didn't fit in. Here at the television company she was the Laura Fisher she had created for herself. Kent brought back memories of an earlier Laura Fisher. One she tried passionately hard not to think about.

FOUR

The day's programme went well by *Newsviews* standards. In other words, there was a varied mix of untaxing items, the presenters smiled a lot, and very few words were spoken unsupported by pictures.

Laura was pleased with her contribution. Lumbered with doing *vox pops* rather than anything more creative, she had produced *vox pops* that stood out. She thought laterally, avoided predictable locations and found unpredictable people to give their opinions on make-up for men. The result, after long and arduous editing through the afternoon, was a very slick little package. The message to Dennis Parker was clear. You give me the boring jobs to do if you like, but I'll still demonstrate my superiority.

In the rush of meeting her deadline and the excitement of the live transmission, Laura had no time to think of the evening ahead. When the *Newsviews* closing credits rolled, it took her a moment to locate the reason for the slight unease within her. Kent. Of course. She rang Reception to see if he was waiting for her. No. She said she could be contacted in the bar, and if they let her know when he arrived, she'd come down to the foyer to meet him. That way she wouldn't have to introduce him to any of her colleagues. She put down the phone and joined the rest of the production team for the usual after-show drinks.

Needless to say, she ended up with Rob. She felt closer to him than anyone else on *Newsviews*. He was more intelligent than the others, for a start. More entertaining, too. And, she had to admit to herself, his sexual orientation lowered the stakes, enabled her to relax with him more than she could with any of the other men on the team.

'So where's Mr Plod?' Rob asked.

'My brother hasn't arrived yet,' Laura replied formally.

'Off investigating a murder perhaps . . . ?'

'Perhaps.'

'Wonder if he's doing this Melanie Harris case . . . ?'

'I don't know.'

'I'll be fascinated to meet him.'

'I'm not sure that he'll be fascinated to meet you.'

'No, of course not.' Rob dropped into a thick copper's voice. ' "I don't want to mix with bloody perverts, me. I'm a straight copper, not a bent copper." ' He chuckled. 'Not that they're all like that, you know. Oh, by no means. I met a *very* interesting Detective Inspector up in a little cottage in Kentish Town . . . and fortunately . . . he'd brought his truncheon with him!'

Rob giggled, covering his face with a hand in

mockery of his own outrageousness. Laura smiled. She never failed to succumb to his awkward child-like charm.

'You're an idiot, Rob. Anyway, I don't think I'll give you the chance to find out what you think of Kent. Soon as they let me know he's arrived, I'll go and meet him at Reception.'

'Don't be such a mean cow. I want to meet him. You say he's not married, don't you?'

'Yes.'

'We-ell . . .' Rob spread his hands wide in a gesture that seemed to encompass all possibilities. 'You never know, I could be what he's been searching for all these years.'

'I somehow doubt it.'

'Stranger things have happened, dear. Look, you and me get on so well together . . . just a pity we're the wrong sex for each other. But if Kent's the male version of you . . . wowee, thunderbolts and lightning *at the very least*.'

'Kent isn't the male version of me. We're very different. We don't have the same . . .' Her words trickled away as she followed Rob's eyeline. Walking towards them, aloof, as if risking contagion from the chattering crowds in the bar, was a tall, solid, rectangular figure in a grey suit and striped tie.

'Mm, now that is *chunky*,' Rob murmured.

Laura rose to her feet. 'Kent. How did you get in? I told Reception to give me a call and I'd come down to meet you.'

Kent Fisher shrugged awkwardly. 'They directed me straight up here.'

'God, the security in this place is so hopeless.'

Sister and brother stood facing each other. There wasn't that much likeness, except in their colouring. His hair was cropped short, and the heavy shadow on his chin suggested his day had started early. They didn't kiss or even hug. Kent would have regarded such gestures as embarrassing showbiz affectation. Besides, theirs wasn't that kind of relationship. They hadn't grown up in an environment where touching was encouraged.

'Well, Laura dear . . .' Rob fluted into the silence, 'aren't you going to introduce me?'

Kent took one look. He noted the tight, long-collared shirt, the velvet trousers, the small diamond finger-ring, and Rob was instantly pigeonholed.

'This is my brother Kent. Rob Sinclair.'

Rob held out — or rather flourished — a hand. Without enthusiasm, Kent reached across and gave it a perfunctory shake.

'*Do* join us for a drink. *Please*. Laura's told me *so* much about you.' Rob sat down and patted the seat beside him. '*Do* sit down and tell me all about what it's like being at the *sharp end* of the battle against crime.'

Laura couldn't decide whether Rob was being more camp than usual or whether he just seemed so in Kent's awkward and forbidding presence.

'Get you a bijou drinkette, Kent?' Rob enquired.

'Well . . .'

'Oh, *go on*. We're going to have another, *aren't* we, Laura darling?'

'Well —'

'*Course* we are.' Rob sprang up again from his seat and asked in a self-consciously butch way, 'What's your poison, Kent old man?'

'Erm, a light ale, thank you.'

Before Laura had time to stop him, Rob scampered away to the bar. She sat down. Kent lowered himself heavily on to the seat beside Rob's, then pointedly moved it away.

'So who's he, Laura?'

'A researcher. Someone I work with on the show.'

'Uhuh.'

Again there was silence between them. Laura felt, as she always did in Kent's presence, younger, immature. She felt she had to justify herself. 'Today's programme went very well,' she said.

'Did it? Ah.'

'You have a good day?'

'Busy.' He didn't volunteer any more.

Laura looked at her brother, and felt a familiar irritation. It was his slowness that always infuriated her, his unwillingness to initiate a conversation. She felt something for him, affection maybe — her upbringing had made her cautious about ever using the word 'love' — but Kent's doggedness had always driven her mad.

Presumably, at work, as a Detective Sergeant, he had to be more forceful, to take the initiative more often. Perhaps it was only she who brought

42

out the reticence in him. But, whatever the reasons for his slowness, it always made her disproportionately angry. She found herself demanding, with more brusqueness than she intended, 'Well, what is it, Kent? Is there some particular reason why you thought it necessary to come and see me here?'

'Yes,' he replied ponderously. 'Yes, there is a reason.' He let one of his aggravating pauses hang in the air, then opened his mouth to continue, but was silenced by the return of Rob sashaying across the bar with one uplifted hand supporting a tray of drinks and the other balanced balletically on his hips.

'Drinkies,' he trilled. 'Drai whaite waine for the lady — and for you, sir, a light ale. I always think light ale's such a *masculine* drink — positively *butch*, don't you agree?'

Kent was totally unqualified to deal with this kind of posturing. His natural instinct — probably to hit its perpetrator — was restrained by the knowledge that Rob was his sister's friend. But he didn't have any other appropriate behaviour to fall back on. With a gruff 'Thank you', he edged further away from the seat into which Rob sank like a wilting lily.

'Oooh, I certainly need this after the day we've had.' Rob held his glass up to the light and swirled around the red fluid with its clinking ice. 'Always Campari for me — with the emphasis on the "Camp".' He brought his knees together and leant forward to Kent in a parody of fascination. 'Tell me,' he said with a flutter of eyelashes, 'have you ever worn make-up?'

'What?' This time it looked as though Kent really would follow his instinct and hit the researcher.

Laura intervened quickly. 'Just we've been doing a feature on it today.'

'On what?'

'Make-up for men.'

Kent snorted and took a long swallow from his drink.

'Apparently it is going to come,' Laura explained. 'And in our feature today a surprising number of the interviewees seemed quite attracted to the idea. Lots of men in the States use it already.'

'Yes, and I can just imagine what kind of men,' said Kent, with an unequivocal look at Rob.

'What, people like *moi,* you mean?' Rob's hands fluttered coyly to his chest. 'True, I'm not quite the Adonis I was a few years back. Anno Domini has taken its cruel toll, I'm not ashamed to admit it. Are you suggesting I might benefit from a dab of the old Max Factor and a flick of mascara? Well . . . I think you could be right.' Rob's face formed into a mask of wistful tragedy. 'Blunt, Kent, cruel perhaps, but — I'm horribly afraid — right.'

The atmosphere didn't improve. Laura kept pleading with her eyes to Rob, but the researcher was enjoying himself far too much and her unspoken entreaties seemed only to goad him to further outrage. Kent became more and more silent, his shoulders more and more rigid.

After a while Laura gave up. She hurried down the rest of her wine and rose to her feet. 'Better be on our way. Are you free for dinner, Kent? We can talk then.'

Kent grunted that he was free.

'I'm free for dinner too,' Rob cooed winsomely.

'Well, bad luck. You're not coming with us.'

A flicker of hurt crossed the researcher's eye, and Laura felt guilty for the brutality of her words. She knew the emptiness of Rob's evenings when he hadn't got anything arranged. But this evening she had to be pitiless. 'I'll talk to you tomorrow,' she hissed at him as they got their coats. 'You're absolutely incorrigible.'

'I know,' the researcher sighed with a defeated gesture. 'I've spent all my life looking for someone to "corrige" me, but have I had any luck? Need you ask?'

As Laura and Kent left the bar, she looked round. Rob lingered, a model of indecision, weighing the options of diving back into the boisterous derision of the *Newsviews* team, or returning to his solitary bedsitter in Kentish Town.

Her brother's body language recoiled from the pastel decor and tall potted plants of the restaurant, but Laura was damned if she was going to change her lifestyle to accommodate his tastes. She knew he would have preferred some honest, traditional place with an English menu and soggy vegetables, but she felt again the perverse desire to antagonize him.

He looked askance at the slim black-clad waiter who flourished menus at them, and his thick eyebrows rose when he saw the contents. 'It's all right,' said Laura. 'My idea — my treat.'

Kent shrugged. He didn't need to say, 'Well, if you choose to waste your money on overpriced Frenchified stuff like this, that's up to you.' His body said it for him.

They ordered. Kent, with a perverseness matching Laura's, insisted on a plain steak without any of the sauces which had helped bring the restaurant and its chef into *The Good Food Guide* for the first time that year. The manner of his insistence contrived — probably as he intended — to put the waiter's back up.

The waiter flounced away and Kent looked at his sister with defiance. Then a great weariness seemed to assail him. His shoulders slumped, tension seeping out of his body, and with the back of his hand he stifled a yawn.

'Long day?' asked Laura, solicitude apologizing for her earlier brusqueness.

Kent nodded. 'Called out at three o'clock this morning.'

'What for?'

'Someone had found a body in a car park.'

'Melanie Harris?'

He nodded.

'She'd been strangled, hadn't she?'

'I don't want to talk about it,' he said with

sudden roughness. More gently, he continued. 'I'm not allowed to talk about it, apart from anything else.'

'No. No, obviously not.'

Kent looked down at his cutlery. He ran a finger slowly along the line of his steak knife. Laura once again felt the irritation well up in her. Why couldn't he just get on with it? Say what he had to say? Why all this bloody preamble every time? But she buttoned her lip and let him make his revelation at his own pace.

'I felt I had to see you,' Kent began slowly. 'Tell you this face to face. Didn't want to do it on the phone.' He was silent again. Two fingers wiggled the steak knife infuriatingly from side to side, but still Laura controlled her annoyance. 'Fact is . . .' Kent finally started again. 'There was a message when I got back into the office this morning.' He stopped and looked up, his eyes locking with hers. 'The old man's dead.'

Laura knew exactly what he meant, but, perhaps to buy time to construct a reaction, found herself asking, 'The old man?'

'Our father,' Kent confirmed. 'He's dead.'

The moment of hearing this news was one that Laura had imagined all her life. But she was still unprepared for the rush of complex emotions which its reality triggered.

FIVE

'**We can't escape** it,' said Kent. A wooden hand-gesture failed to encompass the enormity of what they couldn't escape. 'It's going to be with us all our lives, bound to be.'

Laura shook her head firmly. 'No. We can escape it. I'm not going to let it be with me all my life. I'm making my own life. I've started from scratch, I've remade myself, and I'm not going to allow anything to change the new me.'

Kent sighed and pushed back his unfinished steak. 'I wish I could share your optimism. When I think back . . . there's no way things like that aren't going to affect anyone for the rest of their lives.'

'I don't think back.'

'I try not to, but . . .'

'Come on, Kent, you're strong. You know you are. If you hadn't been strong, I don't think I'd still be here. You protected me . . .'

'And I always will protect you,' he said with sudden fervour.

'I know. I appreciate that very much. But what I've been doing over the last few years is to put myself in a position where I don't need protecting. I want to look after myself.'

'Sure. We all want that. But there are things

48

that happen . . . things that did happen in our lives when we were too small to look after ourselves . . . and I just don't think we'll ever get away from them.'

'I'll get away from them,' Laura asserted. 'I have got away from them. I mean, think what I was like at fourteen . . . sixteen . . . even eighteen. Could you ever imagine then that I'd be holding down the kind of job I am now? Not just holding it down either — doing it bloody well. And I've got the job — and I'm doing it well — simply because I made a decision that that was what I was going to do.'

'Maybe, but —'

'Listen. I decided to join the BBC as a secretary. I decided to pull up my roots and work those six months in New Zealand — in the face of incredible opposition from Michael, I may say. I decided to make the move to ITV when I came back. I decided I wanted to be a director. And that's what I'm now doing. I haven't let anything that happened in the past hold me back.'

'All right,' he conceded. 'All right.' Another of his interminable pauses. 'But you're still scarred by it.'

'No, I'm not. I'm not scarred,' she countered passionately. 'I have healed the scars. I've made myself whole again.'

'Huh.' Kent toyed with his wine glass. 'You must teach me the trick one day.'

'I'd be happy to.'

Despair reasserted its control over him. 'Not

that I think it'd work for me.'

'Why not? Listen, Kent, we're only here for one life. It's not very long. And I'm certainly not going to let my entire life be ruined by things that happened when I was just a kid.'

'It went on way beyond when you were a kid. You were nearly fifteen, remember, when . . . when, you know . . .'

Laura was angry that Kent could not bring himself to say what he meant. Even angrier to discover that she too was unable to put into words the horror they had shared.

'All right, yes, I was nearly fifteen. But that was fifteen years ago. I've got over it.'

'Bully for you,' said Kent with tired disbelief.

'And you've got over a lot of it, too. Come on, Kent, you're holding down a pretty stressful job. You're doing well, you said you're in line for promotion. You haven't let him destroy you.'

'No? Laura, it's one thing to be able to cope at work, it's another to . . .' He shook his head. 'I'm never going to be in a relationship. I've recognized that now.'

'Why?'

He looked at her bleakly. 'Because I'm too afraid of the possibility of history repeating itself.'

'It needn't repeat itself.' Kent looked away. 'Why are you so sure? Things happen. You can change.'

Another defeated shake of the head. 'No. Whenever I've got close to a woman, I . . . Things get complicated . . . So many emotions come into my head that . . .'

It was rare for Kent to reveal so much of himself. Normally he kept his feelings tightly reined in, and Laura could only conjecture what went through his mind. The shock of their father's death had broken down some barrier within him. Kent seemed to realize the singularity of what was happening at the same moment Laura did. His eyes flickered away from hers. When he looked back, their shutters had been replaced.

'So I'm always going to be on my own,' he pronounced without self-pity. Without any emotion, in fact. 'Anyway,' he continued with something that was almost a sneer in his voice, 'your track record on relationships isn't that great, is it? You may be able to be a star in the job, but your personal life —'

'You know nothing about my personal life,' she snapped.

'I know you don't seem to have that many friends.'

'I have enough. A lot of colleagues.'

'Like that mincing poof in the bar?'

'A lot of other friends you don't know. Anyway, some of us don't need people around all the time.'

'I also know,' Kent persisted, 'that your marriage to Michael wasn't much of a success. And I don't think any amount of positive thinking in the world can make you deny that.'

'No. All right. With Michael it was wrong . . . He was the wrong person, it was the wrong time. I was only eighteen, for God's sake. Think back, remember the kind of state I was in when I was eighteen — living with Mr and Mrs Hull — do you remember that? Is it any surprise that the marriage didn't work?'

'No surprise at all. I just wonder why you imagine any other marriage will stand any more chance.'

'Because, as I said, I have changed. I'm my own person now. I could cope with marriage . . . if that was what I wanted.'

'You mean it isn't?'

'I didn't say that,' she replied, suddenly cautious.

'So . . . are you in a relationship at the moment?' This was an unusually direct question, according to the strict rules of circumspection which governed their conversations.

'None of your business,' Laura replied lightly.

'No. No, right.' He accepted the point without argument.

They moved to other topics. Both felt shocked by the intimacy with which they had talked. Though to an outside listener their conversation would have sounded unrevealing, by the conventions of their encounters they had come surprisingly close. Close to talking about the shared secret that was never fully articulated between them.

They did not have much of a range of 'other topics' either. Kent could not talk about his work, and Laura was aware of foot-shuffling resistance from him when she talked of hers. He made her feel as if she was showing off. With so many subjects off-bounds, there was little left to talk about. Neither was particularly interested in the other's views on the Arab–Israeli conflict or the prospective fuel crisis. Relief was felt on both sides when they agreed not to have sweets or coffee and Laura asked for the bill.

She saw her brother wince as she put down two ten-pound notes to cover it, and wince again to see how little change the waiter brought back. Aware again of the perverse desire to annoy Kent, Laura overtipped grotesquely.

Outside the restaurant they stood awkwardly apart in the cold October air. 'I'll let you know about the arrangements,' said Kent.

'Arrangements?'

'Funeral, what have you. I'm sure they'll be in touch when they've sorted it out.'

'Oh, right,' said Laura. 'Fine.'

'Goodbye then.'

'Goodbye.'

Gauchely, without touching, they set off in opposite directions, into their separate lives. They were totally different. Outsiders would have been surprised to know they were even related. Only Laura and Kent knew how much they had in common. She deeply resented the connection, he had perhaps become reconciled to it, but they were inextricably joined by the appalling violence of their upbringing.

The Trimphone warbled in Laura's flat the following Saturday just as she had started nibbling a solitary lunchtime salad. She leant across to the hi-fi and turned down 'Goodbye, Yellow Brick Road.'

'Hello?'

'Laura?'

'Yes?'

'It's Philip.'

The name released a cataract of dammed-up thoughts. Thoughts she'd worked hard to suppress, thoughts which she had disciplined out of her mind and which only broke in as an ache of wistfulness at wakeful three-in-the-mornings when her will-power was at a low ebb.

'Ah. Where are you calling from?' she asked, bleaching her voice of all intonation.

'Heathrow.' This prompted a little surge of hope. Surely it wasn't possible that he had come all this way just to see her? But his next words dashed the hope. 'I'm on my way back to Auckland. Flight'll start boarding in ten minutes.'

'But why . . . ? Have you been over here long?'

'Just a week. Giving a paper at a series of seminars on documentary television.'

The idea of his having been there all week, even having been in London when Laura had her encounter with the man in the hotel, was almost unendurable.

'Just didn't want to leave without saying hello, Laura.' He tried to make the remark sound breezy and unimportant, but she could hear the tension in his voice. 'Why?' she couldn't help asking.

'Why didn't you get in touch with me before?'

'I thought it . . .' The tension was now almost strangling his words. 'I thought it was not right. I thought, safer, if we didn't meet . . . if I just made contact . . .'

'Then why make contact at all, Philip? Are you deliberately trying to hurt me?'

'No. No, I . . . Look, this week's been agony. Every moment that I haven't actually been sitting in meetings and lectures, I've been thinking about phoning you. I've even dialled your number a couple of times, but . . .'

'Oh, Philip . . .'

'It's better this way — really.' The words still struggled out with difficulty. 'This is the right thing to happen.'

'And now you'll be able to sit on that plane for twenty-four hours or whatever it is,' said Laura, a harsh note creeping into her voice, 'congratulating yourself on having resisted temptation once again — is that it?'

'No, no, it's not . . . I'm not scoring points or anything. I'm not trying to hurt you. It's just . . . this is the right thing to happen,' he repeated lamely.

'Right for you perhaps. Right for Julie. Have you ever considered what might be right for me?'

'We went through all this, Laura. We've been through it many times. This is the only way it can be.'

'But don't you still want me?'

'Yes.' He swallowed. 'Yes, I'll always want you.

I still wake up in the night physically hurting from how much I want you, but . . . It can't be any other way.'

'No,' Laura conceded reluctantly. 'How is Julie?'

'Not bad at the moment. Not getting worse, anyway. The doctor says it's probably only a temporary remission, but it could be years before things deteriorate again.'

'That's good. And she's keeping cheerful?' Even as she spoke the words, Laura was aware of their incongruity. Why should she be showing such solicitude for the wife of the only man she had ever loved?

'Yes, yes, not bad at all.'

'And the children?' Again she asked herself why. She didn't care about Philip's children. They were just two more obstacles to her ever sharing her life with him. But as she had the thought, Laura recognized the pattern. It had happened often during their affair. Talking about Julie, talking about the children, had always sobered them up, lowered the temperature, put their relationship in perspective, made it possible for them to part.

'They're great,' Philip replied with distancing bonhomie. 'Paul should be at university next year, with a following wind. And Tammy's actually developed a boyfriend.'

'Good for her.' A meaningless platitude, an automatic response, small talk recognizing the impracticality of any deeper communication.

'So, anyway . . .' Philip's voice continued uneasily, 'I just rang to say hello and see how you are.'

'I'm fine. Directing — and a bit of producing — on *Newsviews*.'

'Yes, I heard. Well done. So you benefited from the experience in New Zealand?'

'Yes,' said Laura.

He was flustered by the deliberate ambiguity in her tone. 'Good, good. And everything else OK?'

'Everything else? You mean my personal life? My emotional life? My sex life?'

This too embarrassed him. His voice was throaty as he replied, 'I've given up any rights to know about your sex life.'

'Yes,' Laura said vindictively, 'you have.' Philip was inarticulately silent. 'Everything's fine, thank you.'

'Good.' He was relieved to have moved back from the brink of further intimacy.

'Oh, Philip . . . I've been through so many conversations with you in my mind.'

'Yes. And I with you.'

'But . . .'

'But this is the only way it can be.' Again he repeated his mantra, the sole article of faith he could cling to. 'This is the right thing to happen.'

'Yes. Yes.'

'Look, they're calling the flight. I must . . .'

'Mm.' Laura, knowing that the flight hadn't really been called, that he just wanted to get off the emotional hook, reverted to polite small talk. 'Well, nice to hear from you, Philip. Do keep in touch, won't you?'

He caught the impersonal tone. 'Yes, yes, of course. And hope all continues to go well for you.'

'And you. Your work still OK, is it?'

'Yes. They've made me head of documentaries, of all things.'

'Congratulations.'

'Thank you. Well, I must . . . Really, the flight . . .'

'Yes.' Suddenly her restraint burst once more. 'Philip, I can't believe I'll never see you again.'

'No, well, I . . . Maybe one day. I must go. Goodbye, love.'

'Goodbye.'

The tone droned in Laura's ear for a full minute before she put the Trimphone down. She pushed her salad to one side and turned up the Elton John. 'Candle in the Wind' mourned away in the background.

Hearing Philip's voice had brought it all back. The iron lid she had crammed down on the whole episode lifted in an instant. She remembered the touch of his skin, even the musky smell of his aftershave.

Her mind filled with that first afternoon when he'd come to her flat. She'd known when she'd seen him in the doorway that they had both been fighting the same impulses. For six weeks they'd each tried to argue them away, tried to convince themselves their feelings weren't reciprocated, that any declaration would only be met by embarrassing incomprehension. Neither had said anything. And they had said little at the beginning of that afternoon. It hadn't seemed necessary. They had just come together, neither one making an advance to the other. Everything had been mutual.

And the love-making that followed had shown the same egalitarianism. For Laura, whose only previous experience of sex had been adversarial, it was a revelation. Compared to Michael's rough and inept pursuit of his own gratification, Philip showed infinite patience and gentleness. For him the touching seemed at least as important as the orgasm. That first time, though time had been a hazy concept while it was happening, it must have been hours before he came. But he used those hours to worship her body, to learn its contours, its triggers, its curves and crevices. His hands, his lips, and just the silky contact of his skin, brought her to levels of pleasure she would not have believed possible. She came and came and came again, and each climax washed away a little more of the accretions of bad sexual experience.

With him it all seemed natural, all continuous, all different. There had been no orders, no compulsion except the mutual desire to touch and be touched. Instinct had taken over. Each seemed to know what the other wanted and when they wanted it. It was not love-making that stopped and started. Michael's sexual offensives all ended with his climax. Then all Laura got was the turned shoulder and a gruff 'Goodnight' or, if it was in the morning, his immediate silent departure from bed to bathroom. But with Philip one encounter flowed seamlessly into the next.

'Where did you learn to be such a wonderful lover?' she had asked in one of the lulls as they lay gently entwined.

'I didn't learn,' he said. 'I've never thought of myself as a wonderful lover. It's only with you. I knew it'd be perfect with you.'

'And I knew it'd be perfect with you. The moment I saw you, Philip, I just knew.'

And it remained perfect. The love-making, that is. They were two people physically designed to complement each other, two people who could never be in the same room without wanting to make love to each other.

But. The old familiar 'but'. Philip was married. He had a wife, Julie, and two small children, Paul and Tammy. He loved them all. It wasn't a case of a man dissatisfied with his wife who was on the look-out for a bit on the side. He loved Julie, but had been totally bowled over by his passion for Laura.

From the start he had made the situation clear. He was not a liar. He told Laura that he had never been unfaithful before, and he was definitely telling the truth. He never pretended that he didn't love Julie or that he would ever contemplate walking out on his family.

He stated all this the second time they were alone together. 'It doesn't mean I don't love you and want you,' he said, 'but there's nothing long-term in it for you, Laura. I'll never leave them. So if you say now that you want me to go and that we'll never make love again, I'll fully understand.'

Laura could no more have said that at that moment than she could have flown. They fell into each other's arms and the second time the love-making was even better.

So the affair continued. They both knew its duration was finite. Laura's contract in New Zealand was only for six months. Then she would have to return to London, and to Michael. But both of them managed to shut their minds to this fact. What was happening was too wonderful, too consuming, for them to look ahead.

In fact the affair ended before Laura went back to England. Two weeks before her departure, Philip's wife Julie was diagnosed to be suffering from multiple sclerosis. The disease was in its very early stages, but, barring some unexpected advance in medical science, it would undoubtedly get worse. Philip, a sensitive and honourable man, was thrown into agonies of guilt by the news. In spite of logic and reassurances from Laura, he could not help seeing his wife's illness as a punishment for his own behaviour. He announced that the affair must end instantly.

Laura, whose love made her far more selfish than he, argued desperately against the decision.

She wouldn't impose on their family life. She would somehow arrange to stay in New Zealand. She wouldn't make demands on Philip, she'd just be there for him. As Julie grew more ill, he'd need her more than ever. But Philip was adamant. He was hurting at least as much as she was. His upbringing, however, left him no alternative but to do the decent thing. Their parting was 'the right thing to happen'.

Even through the sleeplessness of her grief and bereavement, Laura could recognize the irony of the situation. Part of Philip's appeal for her, aside from their sensational physical symbiosis, was his goodness and honesty. It was those qualities, the qualities for which she loved him, that would always keep him supporting his wife and family, and keep him out of Laura's life. Often she wished he had more of the bastard in him, but then a Philip with more of the bastard in him wouldn't be the Philip she loved.

Laura was distressed at how instantly after his phone call all these thoughts had returned, and it required enormous energy over the weekend to reassert her self-control. But by the time she went into the *Newsviews* office on the Monday morning, she was back on track. She was Laura Fisher. She had put the past — all of the past — behind her. And she was going to continue making her own life.

SIX

After the morning editorial meeting the following Thursday Laura lingered while the other producers, directors and researchers filed out. Dennis Parker squinted up at her, his temples tight with that morning's hangover (shortly to be alleviated by a quick slurp from the bottle in his office). A couple of inches of ash hung from the end of his cigarette.

'What?'

'Dennis, I can't be in tomorrow. I've got to take the day off.'

The ash dropped. He brushed it brusquely off his lapel. 'What, women's problems, is it?'

Sometimes Laura could hardly believe the depth of her boss's misogyny. Though he escorted a succession of young actresses around expensive London restaurants — and presumably went to bed with them too — Dennis was one of those men who genuinely hated women. His distaste for the processes of their bodies, particularly for menstruation, was almost pathological. The thought prompted a flicker of excitement in Laura. Her period was due in a couple of days, but she wasn't feeling the familiar bloated restlessness.

'No,' she replied evenly. 'It's my father's funeral.'

'Oh.' Even Dennis couldn't argue with that, but he still managed to come back on the offensive. 'Pity you couldn't have given me a bit more notice. I'll have to reschedule everything.'

Laura knew this to be untrue. Each edition of *Newsviews* was prepared from scratch on the morning of its transmission. Even the designation of the day's studio director could be changed at short notice. But she didn't take issue, simply said, 'I've only just heard the date myself. There had to be a post-mortem.'

'I see.' Even Dennis Parker realized that the situation required some token gesture of condolence. 'I hope you're not too cut up about it — your father . . . "passing on", I mean.' It was odd that someone as professionally blunt should hide behind a euphemism like that.

'No,' said Laura, 'I'm fine. We weren't close.' Though even as she said the words, an involuntary tremor ran through her.

Dennis Parker, realizing he was in danger of being gracious, reasserted his customary boorishness. 'Good. Because the last thing I bloody need is one of my directors sobbing her eyes out over the control desk.'

Laura often wondered what triggered this obsessive hatred of her sex. She generally concluded it was fear.

'And bear in mind,' Dennis added as a parting shot, 'I won't forget. If you ever try to use your father's funeral as an excuse to get another day off work, it won't wash.'

This too was gratuitous offence. Laura had never missed a day since she had started working on the programme. But she knew the pointlessness of taking issue with Dennis on such a detail. He wasn't worth the effort.

'I didn't even know you still had a father,' said Rob that evening, as he looked wistfully through his Campari at her.

'I haven't seen much of him in latter years.'

'No, but you might have mentioned him. Makes me feel very excluded, you suddenly springing a father on me. And I thought I was your *friend.*'

The emphasis showed that Rob was in one of his self-pitying moods. The public flamboyance often gave way to an emptiness bordering on despair. What Laura usually did when she caught him like this was to take him out for a meal and ply him with wine until the alcohol restored at least a façade of giggling outrageousness. But that evening she didn't think she had the energy. The events of the next day were weighing on her mind. She wanted time alone to prepare her reactions to them.

'You *are* my friend,' said Laura, reassuringly rubbing the back of his hand. 'Probably the best friend I've got.'

'And the safest. At least you know I'm not going to spend all my time trying to get inside your knickers.' She acknowledged the truth of this with a little smile. 'Still think you might have told me you had a father, though. I mean, it's not as if I don't tell you *everything* about my mother.'

'That is certainly true.'

'Never guess what the silly bitch did yesterday. Took her filthy smalls down to the launderette and only put *sugar* in the machine instead of soap powder. Honestly, stupid cow isn't safe to be let out on her own.'

The trouble was that his last sentence was true. Through all his bitching, Rob was absolutely devoted to his mother, and though he joked about her advancing senility, it clearly terrified him. How he would react when the old woman finally died Laura did not dare contemplate.

'You going to spring a mother on me too, are you?' Rob asked suddenly.

'No. No, my mother's dead. Died when I was in my teens.' Laura didn't elaborate. Partly this was from instinctive caution, and partly because she did not want to stir up the confused emotions thoughts of her mother always prompted.

There was a silence. Then Rob said dreamily, 'Maybe you and I should get married.'

It was an old joke between them. His sexual orientation and her desire to be single offered the occasional dream of a platonic cohabitation. 'Two old women growing even older together,' as Rob put it, 'bitching about all the men we fucked, and every now and then having furious rows because we wanted to fuck the same one.'

Laura would play along with the joke, but it was Rob's fantasy, not hers. Much as she liked him, she valued her single state too highly to succumb to his possessive presence. Whereas for him the dream did offer an opportunity to stave off the terrible loneliness of the ageing queen.

On this occasion Laura limited her response to an affectionate 'Maybe'.

Rob recognized it as a mild rebuff and looked hurt. He looked even more hurt when, shortly afterwards, Laura drained the last of her wine and said she must be going.

The Friday was markedly colder, one of those face-tingling late October days which bring a sudden reminder of winter's proximity. Kent drove them down from London to Southampton. They took the ferry to the Isle of Wight and went straight to the crematorium.

They said little on the journey. Kent confirmed that he was still working on the Melanie Harris case, but gave no further information.

Laura did not mind the silence. Their shared childhood had not involved many words, a factor which had perhaps strengthened the bond between them. Inside the family home words had been dangerous, words might have prompted painful reactions. And outside their home silence had been the rule, silence about anything that mattered, silence that maintained the myth of middle-class family normality. So being silent with Kent was familiar, even restful. And she felt that being with her gave him some kind of satisfaction which would have been spoiled by words. Words could only emphasize the differences between them, the divergence of their lifestyles and ambitions. Silence bonded.

When they got out of the car at the crematorium, the icy wind slapped at their faces. It carried an invigorating tang of the sea. Laura felt energized. In spite of the appalling memories stirred by the occasion, she experienced an optimism, a sense of change and progress growing within her.

There were few people at the service. The prison governor introduced himself to them and introduced them to a couple of prison visitors, whose rigid smiles bespoke their determination to make the best of the situation, as they had of many other situations. None of the other prisoners had requested permission to attend the service, but then it was unlikely that Richard Fisher would have made many friends during his incarceration.

When the coffin was brought in — a moment Laura had been dreading — she found herself able to look at it dispassionately. The polished wood had become emblematic, anonymous. Whether or not it actually contained the remains of her father, sewn up again after the postmortem, seemed unimportant. He was dead. He had no power to hurt any more. The shiny wooden box held no fears for her.

The optimism within her grew to a positive

glow of well-being. She had escaped the past. The future was hers.

The officiating clergyman, snuffling with a slight cold, maintained the anonymity of the proceedings. As is usually the case when the priest has never met the occupant of the coffin, he restricted his remarks to impersonal platitudes. He emphasized the vague heavenly rewards ahead and concentrated on the generalized good qualities of the deceased. In the second part of this mission, he was more circumscribed than many clergymen in similar situations. What can you say good about a man who abused both his children and was imprisoned for strangling his wife?

SEVEN

His hands were hard and she could feel the hairs on their knuckles as they reached for the elastic of her school knickers and pulled them down. She knew the hopelessness of resistance, but still the repulsion engendered by his flesh, by the object that poked through a frill of Aertex from his unbuttoned tweed trousers, was so strong that her body recoiled and her fists rose instinctively to fight him off.

'Don't you hit me!' her father's voice hissed. 'I'll kill you if you hit me! And I'll kill you if you ever tell anyone about this!'

She froze as he lifted and deposited her without gentleness on to the sofa. Again she felt the tickle of knuckle hairs as he flipped the pleats of her navy school skirt above her waist. Then the hands took firm hold of her upper thighs. She tried as always to detach herself, move the real Laura Fisher away to stand aside and look down dispassionately on what was happening to the other, anonymous Laura Fisher on the sofa.

As he brought his groin towards hers, there was a commotion — the door opening, the dull thud of her father being hit over the head with something. A muffled curse as he turned in fury to face Kent.

The boy in short-trousered school uniform stood his ground while the blows rained into him. Not into his face, nowhere that the marks would show, but hard into the chest and abdomen. Nothing must be seen at school. Nothing must be allowed to make the boy's mother embarrassed to be seen out with him. The façade of middle-class gentility must never be threatened.

Kent let out no sound, but stumbled under the onslaught. Richard Fisher grabbed his son by the shoulders and swung him round like a rag doll. Laura just had time to scramble off the sofa before her brother was slammed face-down on to its cushions. She saw a bead of blood on his lip, and she knew it had not been caused by their father's blows but by the boy's own determination not to allow any cry to escape.

'You get out!' Richard Fisher snarled at her. 'I'll deal with you later.'

Laura did not need a second bidding. She made no attempt to defend Kent — that was not part of their relationship — but, snatching up her knickers, stumbled blindly out of the room. Though she knew the pain it would engender, she could not stop herself from lingering in the hall, the neat middle-class hall with its slightly convex oval mirror, its polished oak telephone-table and anodyne flowered curtains. From inside the sitting room she heard the familiar sounds, the rough accelerating grunts from her father and from Kent the muffled sighs as he bit into his lip to resist the pain.

This was always the worst bit. The sound was more shocking than the sight. She stood frozen, incapable of escape. Her arms would not move to bring her hands up over her ears to shut out the appalling noises.

A tremor ran through Laura's body and she found herself sitting up in bed, nauseous and drenched in sweat. It was a long time since she had had the dream. Since the period of maximum reaction, in her late teens following her mother's murder, it had come less and less frequently. Sometimes, in moments of erupting confidence, she even thought the dream had gone for good. And when, inevitably, it did recur, she was quicker at rationalizing it, more efficient at limiting its after-shock.

She knew what had prompted the nightmare's return. Though nearly a month past, her father's funeral still reverberated through her mind. Laura took a deep breath and contrived, with surprising ease, to force the dream out of her thoughts.

Outside her curtains a thin light glowed. She switched on the bedside light and looked at her watch. A quarter to seven. She swung her legs round to get out of bed. In sitting position she paused for a moment. Her head felt light and the nausea remained. A little surge of excitement told her that reaction to the nightmare was not the reason why she still felt sick.

Cautiously she rose to her feet. Her mouth was dry. She crossed to the kitchenette and took out a packet of coffee beans. But their sharp smell immediately conjured up the metallic taste of vomit in her mouth. Laura returned the packet to the cupboard, filled a glass of water from the tap and, sipping it, went through into the bathroom.

She took off her nightdress and looked at herself in the long mirror. During her teens it had seemed impossible to Laura that she would ever love the body that had prompted so many disgusting encounters. Marriage to Michael had not changed her attitude one iota, though with Philip at times, just for a little while, she had ceased to see herself as dirty and defiled.

Now, as she looked in the mirror, Laura positively loved what she saw. She put her hands to her breasts, cupping them slightly away from the tingling nipples. She ran her hands down her sides, till they rested together on the smooth flatness of her stomach. The nightmare was forgotten. Well-being flooded through her.

She turned to the sink to clean her teeth. As she opened the tube, the peppermint tang of toothpaste rushed up her nostrils. She only just had time to poise herself over the lavatory bowl before she threw up.

Laura knew, but needed formal confirmation. She wished there was some kind of simple do-it-yourself test that could be bought over the chemist's counter, but there wasn't, so she had to go to the doctor.

She knew during the days of waiting for the test results to come back. She had known from the moment she missed her period. Her body had always worked with metronomic accuracy. Even during the worst traumas of her teenage years, the curse had never failed to arrive on time, accurate to the day, almost to the hour.

She rang the surgery at the appointed time and discovered, with very little surprise, that she was officially pregnant.

'Michael's not the father,' said Laura.

'Never occurred to me for one *teensy* moment that he might be.' Rob was in one of his high moods. His voice swooped down dramatically on to individual words. 'You wouldn't want to reproduce anything like *that,* would you?'

'No.'

'So am I going to be let into the *bijou secretette* of who it is?'

'The father?'

'Mm.'

'No.'

'Oh. Oh well, there you go. It's not that you don't know, is it? I mean, you haven't been putting it around so much that it could be virtually any cock in the London telephone directory?'

'No.'

'No, thought not. Not your style, is it, Laura sweetie? Now if it'd been *me* . . .' He spread his hands wide in a gesture of mock-modesty. 'I mean, where would one begin? In the last week

74

alone the candidates must be in double figures. Oh dear, I have been a bit *reckless* recently. Still, what can a chap do? It's the penalty of being absolutely *gorgeous* — something I have to live with. Men just swarm round me — positively *swarm* — bees round a honey-pot . . . and, though I say it myself, a very nice little honey-pot I've got too. No, I think, all things considered, it's just as well there isn't a womb at the end of my arsehole. So many suspects . . . I don't think Hercule Poirot, Miss Marple and Sherlock Holmes, *pooling* their resources, would ever find out whodunnit.'

Laura giggled. Now the doctor had confirmed the news, she felt vindicated. All the planning had paid off. She should give birth in July 1974. As intended, she'd make it before her thirtieth birthday on 4 September. Laura Fisher was once again in control of her life.

'So is the father going to be involved in the child's upbringing?'

'No.'

'Does the father even know that he is to be a father?'

'No,' said Laura.

She phoned Kent the next day to tell him the news. He wasn't at his desk and rang back to her flat in the evening. She told him simply that she was pregnant.

She could feel from his voice the way the shutters had come down, and could visualize the stony deliberate lack of reaction in his eyes. 'Are congratulations in order?' he asked with the minimum of intonation.

'Yes, they are.'

'Congratulations then.' He did not ask for any supplementary information, but apologized that he was busy and would have to get on.

'Still working on the Melanie Harris case? I haven't seen anything in the press about an arrest.'

'Working on that and others,' he replied cagily. 'Must go. Goodbye.'

Laura wondered what her brother really thought about the news. But twenty-nine years of knowing Kent had taught her the impossibility of discovering what actually went on inside his mind.

'Oh, for God's sake!' Dennis Parker downed the remains of his Scotch in one gulp. 'What is the point of employing bloody women? Just when they're beginning to learn something, they get themselves bloody knocked up and suddenly it's all "Oh, I never really wanted a career, anyway. All I really want is to be a wife and mother." '

'That's certainly not true in my case,' said Laura evenly. 'I want a career, too. I'm going to have a child and continue with my career.'

'You'll be lucky. If you think I'm going to have you breastfeeding round the *Newsviews* studio, you've got another thing coming.'

'That will not happen, Dennis.'

'But, look, you're going to be out of action for years.'

'No. I'll work up until the baby arrives and —'

'I'm not that keen on having the *Newsviews* studio turned into a labour ward either, come to that.'

'I will work until the baby arrives,' Laura repeated, 'and then I'll come back six weeks later.'

'You can't leave a six-week-old baby on its own.'

'I will not leave it on its own, Dennis,' she said patiently. 'I will employ a full-time nanny.'

'Huh. And then every time the bloody sprog has a snuffle, you'll be pissing off home early to look after the little bugger.'

'I will not, Dennis. I can assure you that, except for the six weeks I'm away, you will not notice any difference in the amount or quality of work that I put in on *Newsviews*.'

'Hm.' He nodded to the barman for a refill. 'You want anything . . . or don't you think you should be drinking *in your condition?*'

She didn't actually want a drink, but, to counter the sneer in his voice, asked for a dry white wine. It tasted oddly acid on her tongue.

Dennis took a big swallow from his Scotch. 'And what makes you think I'll keep your job open for the six weeks when you choose to go off and have a baby?'

'I think you'll find that you're contractually obliged to, Dennis.'

'I don't give a shit about contracts. I'm editor

of *Newsviews* and if I want someone off the team I get them off.'

'I'm sure you do, but you don't want me off the team.'

'Why not?'

'Because I'm good.'

'Modest too, I see,' Dennis snorted.

'Modesty or lack of modesty doesn't come into it. I just have an accurate assessment of my own abilities. I know how many ideas I contribute to the programme, and I know you'd get a lot fewer good ones if I wasn't there.'

'Huh. There are other people around with good ideas.' But he didn't pursue it. Tacitly he had accepted her point. He chuckled. 'Must say it's a bit of a turn-up. Didn't think Michael had it in him. I'd assumed he'd been firing blanks all these years.'

Laura was surprised Dennis didn't know she was living apart from her husband. They were both members of the same continuation-of-public-school gentlemen's club and she knew they met there from time to time. On reflection, though, she realized how characteristic it would be of such masculine encounters for nothing personal to be discussed, and also how typical of Michael it would be to maintain the front that nothing was wrong with his marriage.

Dennis's words reminded her, though. Michael would have to be told about her condition. And she didn't particularly look forward to his reaction.

EIGHT

After their father was arrested for murdering their mother, the Fisher children were put into care. For a few weeks, while the authorities still reeled from the shock of what had happened, the two were in separate establishments, but Kent's behaviour was so disruptive that, on the advice of the psychologist monitoring their case, they were quickly reunited. Kent was then fifteen, and Laura fourteen.

A series of short-term fostering experiments led to the children finally being placed with a Mr and Mrs Hull. The couple had tried to persuade Kent and Laura to call them something less formal, but without success. In both children's minds they always remained 'Mr and Mrs Hull'.

They were a well-meaning childless couple, whose attempts to break through their charges' reserve never stood a chance. Kent and Laura were too traumatized to begin to trust anyone, and the style of Mr and Mrs Hull's earnest overtures to them could not have been less calculated to appeal. The foster parents had been carefully matched to the social background of the children, but Kent and Laura knew only too well what could be hidden behind a façade of middle-class gentility and did not give the Hulls the smallest comfort of their confidence.

After they had left their foster home, neither child attempted to make further contact. Mr and Mrs Hull valiantly phoned and wrote encouraging letters for a couple of years, but then gave up the hopelessly one-sided desire for communication. They consigned their relationship with the two children to the catalogue of other disappointments that had been their lives, and comforted themselves with the thought that they had at least given Kent and Laura practical help during 'a very difficult period'. All things considered, the two young people had 'turned out pretty well'.

This had also been the view of the psychologist a few months after the children had started living with the Hulls. Once reunited with his sister, Kent's behaviour had improved instantly. He had buckled down to work at his new private school and, to everyone's surprise, performed creditably at 'A'-Level. He did not say a great deal, but then he had never been a communicative child. And not even his sister knew much about what went on behind his dull, ungiving eyes.

Kent's decision to go into the police force had first been formulated soon after his mother's murder. Whether the investigation of her death had stimulated the boy's interest in police work, or whether its injustice had prompted him to devote his life to the battle against crime, was impossible to know. Such confidences were among the many that Kent never released.

On his nineteenth birthday he started at Hendon

Police College, and during the basic course showed himself to be a doggedly efficient if unspectacular student. From the moment he began training, he moved out of Mr and Mrs Hull's house and stayed out, not even returning for Christmas. He still kept in touch with Laura, taking her out every couple of weeks for a meal. On these occasions he would say little, while Laura might chatter or, more often, allow the restful silence to extend between them. She felt, as she had felt all her life, that Kent was there to protect her. The fact that he was now in uniform only reinforced that feeling.

Laura's difficulties in growing up with the Hulls were different from Kent's. Mrs Hull, who had always wanted a daughter of her own, attempted to fit Laura Fisher into this preordained mould. She would take the girl off on generous shopping trips and try to engender an atmosphere of all-girls-together matiness between them. Nothing could have appealed to Laura less, but Mrs Hull seemed unaware of the girl's repeated recoil from intimacy. The older woman went on confiding and giving herself, perhaps in the expectation that Laura would eventually follow her example and open up a little. It was a forlorn hope.

Mrs Hull, without children of her own, also had a slightly dated notion of morality. She still subscribed to the fifties view that teenage girls must be rigidly chaperoned to protect them from the predatory intentions of teenage boys. As a result, Laura was guarded as rigidly from romantic adventure as any medieval princess locked up in a castle.

Laura did not enjoy this. It was not that she had any desire for sexual experimentation — her early experiences had left her numbed and apathetic — but she did resent the curbing of her freedom. The control her father exerted over her life had been inescapable, but she did not see why she should submit to similar restraints from a woman who had, in Laura's view, nothing to do with her.

Mrs Hull had a strong will, however, and an equally strong determination to produce as her own a young woman of impeccable social demeanour. To this end, Laura was groomed and educated as a young lady should be. She completed her education at a socially correct girls' private school, where she was totally indifferent to the social and sexual aspirations of her class-mates; and was then sent to an upper-class secretarial college, where her fellow-students inspired in her the same lack of interest.

But she could not help noticing how much more freedom the other girls had. They were sharing flats, even in some cases moving in with boyfriends. They were allowed to behave as grownups, while Mrs Hull still insisted on Laura living at 'home' and seemed to keep a continual surveillance on her. Whether this protectiveness arose from Mrs Hull's knowledge of her charge's troubled past, or from fulfilment of the fantasy of her own perfectly behaved daughter, Laura neither knew nor cared. She had no emotional reaction to Mrs Hull, simply a resentment of the way the older woman restricted her freedom.

In retrospect, Laura could not understand why she hadn't just walked out. It would have been easy enough. At first Kent would have helped her out financially — he had frequently offered to do so — and then she could have got a job and never seen Mrs or Mr Hull again. But at the time she had had no will. Looking back on it, Laura decided that for the four years after her mother's murder she had been in shock. She had felt emotions and resentments, but all through a gauze of apathy. She had wanted to break away from the Hulls, she had felt chafed by the way her foster mother circumscribed her life, and yet the effort of doing anything to change her situation had seemed insurmountable.

So she had done what was expected of her, nodded, smiled, fallen in with Mrs Hull's arrangement of her social life, while all the time a dormant pilot light of anger glowed quietly within her. That her compliant performance had been convincing could be judged by the Hulls' reaction when she finally stated that she didn't want to see them again. For the couple this desertion was a totally unexpected body-blow; for Laura it was a logical step she had been contemplating from the first moment she met them.

The escape from Mr and Mrs Hull's smothering gentility, however, had been effected according to their rules. By her foster mother's somewhat dated standards, the only respectable reason for a daughter to depart the parental home was to get married. Laura was eighteen, young perhaps by middle-class standards to embark on matrimony, but it was Mrs Hull's view that such a step might 'settle' the girl.

So Laura had been introduced to Michael Rowntree with marriage in mind — at least in Mrs Hull's mind. He had been selected as the son of a family she knew, as someone who had been to the right schools and who was already a partner in a rather condescending West End estate agents. He had been appropriately stunned by Laura's beauty, to which the dazed state of her late teenage years gave an additional, appealing fragility.

He took her out the appropriate number of times, planted an appropriate number of kisses on her numb lips, and at the appropriate time proposed to her. Laura had no recollection of the moment when she consented to his offer, but Mr and Mrs Hull had been delighted by the outcome and instantly turned the ignition key on the Centurion tank of wedding preparations. From that moment, doubts and anxieties were swept aside; nothing could halt the tank's inexorable progress to the altar of middle-class convention. Mrs Hull was delighted that, after the 'difficulties' of her upbringing, Laura's life had 'turned out so well', and she felt quietly proud of the contribution she and her husband had made to that progress.

In keeping with the sweet, old-fashioned values of the Hulls, Michael and Laura did not sleep together before they were married. The reasons for this had in fact nothing to do with the foster parents' wishes. Laura, who had long ago simply sealed over that part of her mind which contained memories of her father's abuse, had no interest in sex. And Michael, who was spoiled by the devotion of a possessive mother and whose early carnal encounters had all been with prostitutes, was one of those dangerous men who set the women they were to marry on a pedestal. Commercial sex had been a grubby, secretive transaction; sex with his wife would be a thing of beauty and purity, almost a sacrament.

Given the widely divergent attitudes with which the newly-weds had approached the event, it was not surprising that their wedding night had been a total disaster.

Laura could not help thinking back to that night as she sat opposite Michael in the restaurant she had chosen for their potentially awkward encounter. It was an American hamburger joint, recently opened, with uncovered wooden floors and dark bentwood chairs. On screens set high up the walls, silent films flickered. The menu featured such phrases as 'animated by the tang of dill', 'caressed with garlic butter' and 'embosomed in soft Swiss cheese'. The waiters were — or at least sounded like — sassy New Yorkers and flirted with diners of both sexes. Laura knew Michael would hate it. She wasn't certain why she had set out to antagonize him from the start. Perhaps she hoped his disapproval of the venue would dilute his fury at the news she had to tell.

'Not as if we haven't got enough bloody American influences here already,' he had complained predictably enough when he arrived. 'Why don't they bloody stay home and sort out their own messes? God, we don't want to take anything from a country which has a bloody shyster for a President.'

The waiter arrived with a bottle of wine. Michael looked at Laura. 'What the hell's happening?'

'I ordered it.'

'Oh, did you?' Ungraciously he took the bottle from the waiter and looked at it. 'God, this is some bloody Californian gnat's piss. You shouldn't let them take advantage of you like this, Laura. You should have waited till I got here to order.'

'This is what the lady asked for,' the waiter said perkily.

'Well, the lady doesn't know anything about wine, so take the bloody bottle away and get us something decent. Presumably you do do French wine?'

'Oh, certainly, sir,' replied the waiter, imperturbably polite, and fanned a cardboard menu in front of Michael.

'That.' He stabbed at the list. 'And make it quick.'

Laura wondered how she had ever convinced

herself that this man would make a suitable husband. Within thirty seconds of any meeting he
had the ability to make her instantly grateful for
their separation.

Again she thought back to the awfulness of
her wedding night. In a way, though, it had been
a blessing. That shock had begun the process of
waking her from her long trauma. It had been
a necessary part of her development.

Michael looked derisively round the restaurant.
'God, what a bloody gimmicky place. I suppose
this is the kind of thing *television people* go for,
is it? The new trendy place, eh?'

'It's convenient, and the burgers are good,' said
Laura.

'Huh. Overpriced foreign rubbish. Just another
symptom of what's happening to London, a place
like this. Bloody foreigners everywhere. Bond
Street'll soon end up looking like a Middle Eastern
bazaar. You can't walk two steps without bumping
into a bloody Arab.'

'I'm surprised you complain. I thought it was
the 'bloody Arabs' who were buying all your expensive properties.'

'That's true. And very grateful to them we
are. Helping us over a potentially sticky patch.
Not that it'll go on like this. Market'll soon pick
up. You can never go wrong in the long term
with bricks and mortar. Oh no. I don't mind
bloody Arabs buying the places, but I'm buggered
if I actually want them living here.'

The waiter arrived with another bottle of wine,

which Michael again grabbed and inspected suspiciously. 'Looks all right. I'll want to taste it. Presumably you're not used to customers asking to do that in a place like this?'

'We always pour wine to be tasted, sir,' replied the waiter, unfailingly courteous. He drew the cork, wiped the bottle's neck with a cloth and neatly decanted a little into Michael's glass. Michael took a sip and grudgingly admitted that the wine was all right.

'Are you ready to order yet, madam? Sir?'

'I've only just bloody arrived, haven't I?' Michael picked up the large, colourful menu. 'Give us five minutes.'

'Certainly, sir.'

The waiter withdrew. Michael followed his departure with narrowed eyes, then looked down at the menu. 'God, I hate being taken for a ride in places like this. You're only paying for the gimmicks, you know.'

'As a matter of fact,' said Laura evenly, 'the prices here are very reasonable. And I'm paying, anyway, so it's not your problem.'

'And no doubt if I did insist on paying, I'd be condemned yet again as a Male Chauvinist Pig, wouldn't I?'

'Yes,' said Laura.

'Oh, God, what's happening in this country? Everything's bloody arse-about-tit. Men are no longer allowed to behave like men, women have completely lost their femininity, the place is being taken over by bloody Yanks and Arabs. And now we've even got the Arabs messing up our fuel supplies. Do you know, I had to queue for nearly an hour to get a full tank of petrol this morning?'

'Yes, we've done a few features for *Newsviews* on what's going on at the pumps.'

'Really? Well, I'm sure those must've been jolly interesting. Sorry I missed them.' His voice was heavy with sarcasm. He turned his attention to the menu. 'So . . . let's see if they do anything mildly edible.'

He huffed and puffed disapprovingly through the list of hamburgers, then called the waiter across and elaborated his demands for a plain rare steak 'without any of that filthy garnish muck on it'. One of the very few tastes he and Kent had in common.

While Michael detailed his demands, Laura found her mind going back again to their wedding night. She had known what was required of her as a bride and, had her new husband shown even the smallest gesture of tenderness, might have overcome the revulsion for male flesh that her father's actions had generated within her. But Michael's only experiences — of masturbation and, with prostitutes, its interactive equivalent — gave him no consideration for a partner's feelings.

His first assault had met unexpected resistance. Following the sniggered after-lights-out dormitory advice that women always mean 'yes' when they say 'no', he had made a second attack which was near to rape. When Laura had managed, with

89

difficulty, to repulse this, he had lost his nerve, and with it his erection. He had stormed out of their Mayfair hotel room and apparently spent most of the night walking the streets of London in fury.

They had left the next day for a honeymoon in the south of France. By the end of two weeks there, a kind of sex life had been evolved. Michael had agreed to be less violent in his approaches, and Laura had agreed to submit to them. She expected no pleasure from this compliance, and got none, but it was what her married state required of her. For Laura pleasure and fulfilment from sex were to wait until she met Philip.

As she looked at her husband across the table, as she heard him patronizing the waiter, Laura felt again the awkwardness, the sheer embarrassment, of their wedding night. She should have got out of the marriage right there and then. But she had still been numb, still half-there, still lacking the self-worth that could have given her the impetus to escape. So she had gone through the agonies of the relationship.

Once again, as it had been with her mother, as with Mr and Mrs Hull, the main priority for Michael seemed to be the preservation of a middle-class façade of happiness. Nothing made him more furious than the suspicion that Laura might have confided to someone any doubt about the perfection of their marriage. It was when Michael feared some such lapse or deception had been perpetrated that he was most likely to hit his wife. Then, and on those increasingly frequent occasions when drunkenness rendered him impotent.

Laura's crawl out of the marriage had been long and slow. First, against her husband's wishes, she had taken a job. She had not told him of her application to work as a secretary at the BBC, simply announced the appointment when she was accepted.

The job had broadened Laura's horizons, not only revealing creative skills and kindling professional ambitions within her, but also bringing her into contact with a lively variety of other women. Their relaxed attitude to relationships, and their lack of reticence in discussing them, made Laura question even more the advisability of her own marriage. Though she still held back from getting too close to any of these women, their influence was enormous.

The six-month contract in New Zealand had been the big break. Michael, needless to say, had made an incredible fuss about the suggestion and had tried everything in his power to stop Laura from going. He had even at one point hidden her contraceptive pills and tried to rape her into pregnancy. But Michael's power over his wife was diminishing. As her own confidence grew, she saw the fragility of his, and came to recognize his bluster for what it was — a mask for an ineffectual spirit and a frightened soul.

The New Zealand episode had achieved what she had hoped for professionally, broadening her experience and putting her in a position to apply confidently on her return for a job as researcher on *Newsviews*. Meeting Philip and discovering the potential of her sexuality had been a glorious bonus. But a bonus which, she soon came to recognize, could lead nowhere. Philip would never leave his wife, and Laura would never put the pressure on to try and make him. If she wanted a family life of her own, she would have to create it herself. On her own terms. Which was what she had done.

And now it was time to announce — not explain, announce — the situation to the man whom she unhesitatingly thought of as her ex-husband. In the same way as when she had left Mr and Mrs Hull, Laura's mind had long been made up that she would leave Michael. And, as it had been with the Hulls, she could not understand why Michael was taking such a long time to come to terms with the idea.

She ordered a hamburger, 'variegated with strips of crunchy bacon and drenched in tangy blue cheese'. When the waiter had gone, she moved straight on to the purpose of their meeting.

'Michael,' she announced, 'I'm pregnant.'

'What?' His first reaction seemed to be pleasure. Maybe he had hoped so many times to hear those words from her that logic was momentarily suspended. But the next second his face clouded. 'What! But you and I haven't slept together for over a year.'

'I am fully aware of that.'

'But . . . You mean you've . . . ? You little slut!' Laura was silent, waiting for the storm to blow itself out. 'You little whore! Who is he? You tell me who he is!'

'It's not relevant.'

'Not relevant? Not relevant who my wife is committing adultery with!' His voice was getting louder. People at adjacent tables stirred in that distinctively British embarrassment which is prompted by any kind of scene. 'Are you living with the bastard?'

'No.'

'Then why the hell . . . ? Why did you let yourself get knocked up?'

'I didn't let myself get knocked up. I chose to become pregnant.'

Realizing the notice he was attracting, Michael lowered his voice and leant forward to Laura. 'You can get rid of it,' he murmured. 'It's not so difficult to arrange these days. There's a chap I play cricket with who got his girlfriend in the club and —'

'I am going to keep the baby,' said Laura coolly. 'I just knew you'd find out about it some time and thought it better you should hear the news from me.'

'You "thought it better I should hear the news from you"?' Michael hissed. 'You cuckold me with some worthless fucker and you "think it better I should hear the news from you"?'

Again she was silent. Suddenly Michael lost control. And seemed to lose the volume control on his voice at the same moment. 'You little cunt!' he screamed.

Laura realized the drawback of her choice of venue. In a restaurant he despised as much as this one, Michael didn't care about drawing attention to himself. She should have chosen somewhere more formal, some regular haunt where he was known perhaps. Better still, she should have asked him to take her to his club, where women, only admitted to certain rooms and at certain hours, were made fully aware of the enormous privilege accorded them in being allowed to share overcooked nursery food with its members.

Still, too late for such thoughts. She'd just have to let his anger run its course. Michael hurled abuse at her for a little longer. The other diners did that very British thing of averting their faces, as though the shame was theirs.

The wind was suddenly gone from Michael's sails. He sank wearily back on to his bentwood chair. An almost audible sigh escaped from the other diners. It seemed that the awkwardness might be over.

'You realize this means I'll have to divorce you, Laura,' he said.

She sighed patiently. 'That's what I've been asking you to do for years.'

The thought of divorce had sobered him. 'It's a big step,' he ruminated. 'Nobody in my family has ever been divorced.' He looked up at her with sudden magnanimity. 'Tell you what, Laura,

94

we'll forget this has ever happened.'

'What on earth do you mean? We can't forget I'm pregnant. I *am* pregnant.'

'I mean, forget about your . . . lapse. Pretend *that* never happened.' She looked at him curiously, still unable to catch his drift. 'For God's sake, Laura, I'm making you an offer very few husbands in the world would make. I'm saying we'll forget the . . . circumstances of your pregnancy.' He straightened up. His jaw was outlined by nobility. 'I'm saying I'm prepared to bring up the baby as our own.'

It was a second or two before she could reply. Then, slowly, patiently, Laura said, 'That is not what I want, Michael. The decision to get pregnant was mine. The decision to bring up the child on my own is also mine. None of it has anything to do with you. So far as I am concerned, Michael, I have no desire ever to see you again.'

This time he really did go berserk. He grabbed the wine bottle like a club and advanced on her. She had to be rescued by the waiters, who pinioned his arms. Only when they had actually called the police did Michael break free and hurry off out of the restaurant.

The other diners cleared their throats, started light conversation and studiously avoided looking at Laura. She ate her hamburger and drank the entire bottle of wine.

NINE

Laura didn't get any more trouble from Michael.
For a few days she walked around in fear, even
going to the extent of carrying in her handbag
the gun she had procured when doing the *Newsviews* feature on illegal firearms. But her husband
made no attempt to accost or even contact her.

When she calmed down, Laura could see the
logic of this. For someone of Michael Rowntree's
conventional outlook, her pregnancy really would
be the final straw to break the back of their marriage. She reckoned the next time she would hear
from her husband would be through his solicitors.
In spite of this, she could not lose the old feeling
that Michael was spying on her. More than once
she thought she'd glimpsed him in a crowd, following her at a distance. But maybe she was imag-
ining it. She felt so ghastly, on the edge of nausea
most of the time, that paranoid visions might well
be another symptom of her general malaise.

She had hoped to have the kind of pregnancy
in which the mother-to-be glowed throughout,
given new energy and certainty by her condition.
Instead, Laura felt positively ill for the first three
and a half months. She threw up every day on
waking, and had to make many unscheduled —
and deviously explained — rushes to the Ladies

during the day. All the time she felt lumpish, drained and as if she was about to succumb to gastric flu.

What made the situation more difficult was her determination not to let anyone on the *Newsviews* team see how she was suffering. This was sensible with regard to the men, particularly Dennis, for whom the slightest lapse from health or good humour would provide a cue for more misogynistic gibes, but Laura also kept the way she felt from her female colleagues. This was instinctive. Although she got on perfectly well with them in a work context, she didn't have any close women friends. Only to Rob, at the end of a particularly heavy day, might she now and then let the mask slip and hint at how wretched she was feeling.

But the wretchedness was purely physical. Never for a moment did Laura question the wisdom of the decision that had put her in this position. It was still part of her life-plan, and the knowledge that she would now achieve motherhood before the deadline of her thirtieth birthday never failed to prompt a little surge of confidence and satisfaction.

In the fourth month of her pregnancy, Laura suddenly felt better. The change was instant and, though brief moments of nausea recurred, she knew the worst was over. The improvement started on the sixteenth of February. It was a Saturday so, after getting up to make a cup of tea — she still couldn't tolerate the aroma of coffee — and pick up the post, Laura allowed herself the luxury of a lie-in. In the cocoon of sheets and blankets she felt secure, and it was a while before the realization trickled through that she didn't want to throw up.

The improvement in her mood was boosted by the receipt of a Valentine. Two days late, but it was always hard to judge the posts right from New Zealand. 'I will love you always,' the printed message read, and Laura believed it. Underneath Philip had scribbled, 'It was wonderful to hear your voice.'

In a way, the inadequacy of the message had a calming effect. It seemed to encapsulate the hopelessness of their relationship, and the impossibility of its ever being more than it was. The occasional card, perhaps now and then a snatched, awkward phone conversation — that was all that could be hoped for.

Laura had recognized this truth long before, but perhaps only recently had she fully accepted it. Her decision to get pregnant had been one of the consequences of that acceptance. So now, though Philip's card brought a pang, it was not the old anguish. Now it was a kind of melancholy, a rueful recognition of the untidiness of a world in which the obvious harmonies are not achieved and the loose ends are never adequately tied up. Laura Fisher had put all thoughts of Philip behind her, and was moving on.

She was also, she knew, doing her job better than ever. Through all the discomforts of early pregnancy, she had raised her work-rate, endlessly scouring her brain for new ideas and ways of enlivening old formats. She was determined to prove her worth to Dennis, partly so that he would have no excuse for blocking her return to *Newsviews* after the birth; and partly because she was damned if she was going to give him any prompts for disparaging put-downs about hormones.

At work she told everyone that the baby's estimated time of arrival was late August 1974, a month later than the real date. She reckoned that this precaution would save her from over-zealous solicitude as her time grew near.

'Thank God I haven't got your job,' said Laura. 'Don't somehow think I could do it.'

The vision mixer, a pretty girl in her thirties, grinned back. In the Control Cubicle other production staff shifted in their seats, twitchy with pre-transmission nerves. Laura, in a voluminous Indian print dress, sat awkwardly, dwarfing a swivel chair. The distended belly that would have prevented her from reaching the vision mixer's controls swelled massively in front of her, so that the only comfortable posture she could find was with her legs apart.

Even then 'comfortable' was a relative term. The aching in her back had been continuous for the previous month. And in spite of the studio's air conditioning, Laura could feel the sweat trickling down to the waistband of her knickers. On a table beside her stood a glass jug and paper cup of water, from which she kept sipping. She didn't look forward to having to go out into the sticky July evening when the programme and the inevitable after-show drinks ended.

She was studio director that Friday. Dennis, characteristically, seemed to take delight in testing her, building up the pressure, looking forward to the moment when she would refuse one of the duties he imposed on her, 'because of her condition'. Laura, equally characteristically, took on everything he offered and determined to show him just how well she could do it.

Studio director was the most stressful job on *Newsviews*. Whoever had the role was completely in charge of the programme's live transmission, with responsibility for cutting off interviewees when they became boring, deciding which items to move up the order, which to drop and which to edit down while on air. The studio director had also to be alert for news stories which might break during transmission, necessitating the sudden summoning of correspondents and instant rejigging of the running order.

All this had to be fitted exactly into a forty-five-minute slot with two commercial breaks. Any errors of timing would lead to complaints across the ITV regions from the advertisers who did not get the full air-time they had paid for.

All live television programmes are tense and, although *Newsviews* was essentially a lightweight show, Dennis Parker's journalistic machismo demanded that the atmosphere in the studio every evening should be positively frenetic. The schedule would have been stressful enough anyway, but Dennis's presence always added an additional strain. Though the studio director was nominally in charge, the editor was perfectly capable of countermanding — and indeed likely to countermand — his or her decisions and demand, while they were on the air, major changes from the prepared running order. Sometimes these changes were for sound journalistic reasons; more often, Laura had long since concluded, Dennis was simply flexing his muscles and showing who was in charge.

As ever, he was in the Control Cubicle that evening, standing just behind her. She knew that, once they went on air, his belly would start to bump rhythmically against her chair, jarring her already aching back. He always did that during transmission. Some of the team reckoned it was an involuntary nervous habit; Laura knew Dennis to be fully aware of how annoying the mannerism was.

'OK, good luck, studio. Good luck, everyone,' said Laura. 'Start the clock.' And they counted down the beginning of that evening's *Newsviews* live into the ITV network.

For some reason the programme was a particularly tough one. Two politicians almost came to blows in one interview and another of the studio guests suddenly got camera fright and became almost incapable of speech. The link with Spain broke down in the middle of a correspondent's live report about General Franco's hand-over of power to Prince Juan Carlos.

Laura rode all these crises with aplomb, though they were made more critical by conflicting orders from Dennis. As tension in the studio mounted, the tapping of his stomach against her chair became more like a drumming. That day's *Newsviews* was a very long forty-five minutes.

When the credits had finally rolled to their end and in different regions different commercials had started, the vision mixer, sweat gleaming on her brow, pushed a control and faded to black. Laura leant uncomfortably forward and pressed down the talkback key. 'Thank you, studio. Well done, everyone. Buy you all a drink in the bar.'

It was the movement that made her aware of the wetness on the inside of her legs. Instantly she realized what had happened. Just at that moment the waters had broken. The baby had started. As if to reinforce this message, she felt a sudden breath-draining spasm in her stomach. Oh my God, she thought, a contraction.

Surreptitiously Laura looked down to the green institutional carpet. A pool of fluid was spreading round the front wheels of her swivel chair. Close behind her she could hear Dennis congratulating himself on how well he'd dealt with the programme's crises. She was damned if he was going to know what had happened. She could imagine how long he would make ammunition like that last in his misogynist joke offensive.

In one movement Laura rose to her feet and swept over the water jug, so that it spilled down her skirt and on to the floor. 'Oh, bugger!' she said.

'No need for language like that,' Dennis reproved. 'Don't like to hear ladies swearing.' Laura had only a moment to reflect how typical such nicety was of his chauvinist double standards before the editor seized the opportunity for another gibe. 'Getting a bit clumsy, are you? Gather that happens quite often in pregnancy.'

'Not getting clumsy, Dennis, just getting big. A stomach like mine is virtually an offensive weapon.'

He looked smug. 'Well, you said it.'

Laura stole a glance down at the floor. It was all right. The water from the jug had mingled with the existing pool. 'See you all in the bar,' she repeated, and moved swiftly but gingerly out of the Control Cubicle.

Fortunately there was no one else in the Ladies. She mopped herself up as far as was possible, then was almost immobilized by another shuddering spasm. She tried to remember what her book on pregnancy had said about frequency of contractions. Maybe she should abandon her team and get herself to the hospital as soon as possible.

But no. She wouldn't give Dennis the satisfaction. The *Newsviews* studio director's job wasn't finished until drinks had been bought for all the studio guests and crew.

Breathing deeply and concentrating hard, Laura

Fisher left the Ladies and took the lift up to the bar. There, supporting herself against the counter, she waited as the programme team trickled in, and relayed to the barman their shipping order of drinks. She passed Dennis his customary quadruple Scotch and, although she had gone off the taste of alcohol, ordered a dry white wine. She knew she was sweating and steeled herself against the pain of another contraction.

'Feeling all right, are you?' asked Dennis with patronizing solicitude. 'Look a bit wan.'

'Fine. You just feel the heat a bit more when you're the size of a house.'

'I would imagine so. Still, got the weekend to relax, eh?'

Somehow Laura thought relaxing was the last thing she would be doing over that weekend, but she didn't say so, just nodded. She'd ring on the Monday to tell them she wouldn't be in. Surely the baby would have arrived by then.

She winced as another contraction ripped through her. Still three or four minutes apart, but they seemed to be getting closer. She looked at her watch. Twenty past seven. Quarter to eight was the earliest the studio director could legitimately leave the bar without raising comment.

She gritted it out. Her back now ached so much that she wondered whether she would be able to stand without the support of the bar. Every now and then the pain of another contraction seared through her. But all the time she kept up the post-studio small talk, flattering the guests about their performances, joshing with the crew about disasters just averted.

Rob swanned across towards her. '*Lovely* show, sweetie, *lovely*. Dahling, you were absolutely *fantabulous*.' Anxiety came into his eye as her face twitched from another contraction. 'Are you all right, Laura?'

'Fine. Just hot and uncomfortable, that's all.'

'Not surprised. I'd be uncomfortable if I was walking around with a mahogany sideboard under my shirt.' Again he looked anxious. 'Sure you're OK? Sure there's nothing I can do?'

'Quite sure. Well, actually . . . could you ask Esther to organize a cab for me? At ten to eight.'

'Where to? Home?'

'Er, no. Goldhawk Road.' She hadn't said 'Queen Charlotte's Hospital', but Rob still looked at her curiously. 'Supper with a friend there,' she explained.

'Anyone I know?'

'No, and I'm certainly not going to introduce him to you. He's far too pretty. I'm not having you whisking him off to bed.'

'Well, I don't envy him whisking *you* off to bed.' He pointed to her stomach, which trembled with yet another convulsion. 'Honestly, however randy they were, I don't think anyone could *find* anything very interesting under that lot.'

Laura managed to chuckle and Rob moved away, untroubled, to fix her cab. It was all right. He had been put off the scent and their usual insulting badinage had been re-established.

She made it till a quarter to eight, then, with a series of elaborately casual goodbyes, managed to leave the bar. In her office, hidden away from prying eyes in a filing cabinet, was the suitcase she had prepared for this moment.

She felt more contractions in the lift on the way down. The cab was waiting. Once again she just said, 'Goldhawk Road'. The cabbie mercifully was not one of the chatty kind. 'Here,' she said as they passed the gates of Queen Charlotte's Hospital.

It was only when she got out to pay him and winced at the pain of another contraction that the driver seemed to notice her condition. ' 'Ere,' he asked with disappointment in his voice. 'You're not in labour, are you? 'Cause I could've really hurried, you know, if I'd known — blaring the hooter, lights flashing, the lot.'

'No,' said Laura. 'Just here for a check-up.'

He looked even more disappointed.

She checked in and was escorted directly to the labour ward. The sister who took her details tried to disguise it, but Laura was aware of a slight sniff of censure. Even in 1974 there were professionals who disapproved of single motherhood.

TEN

He was the most beautiful baby in the world. Laura was amazed by how immediately she slipped into the cliché of every new parent. But, in spite of the instinctive, protective detachment that normally kept her at a cynical distance, she couldn't deny it was true. Tom was the most beautiful baby in the world.

Immediately after the birth, she was surprised by two things. First, by how instantly, in spite of the long hours of unprecedented pain she had just been through, how instantly she had loved him. And second, by how separate Tom seemed. He was apart from her, his little eyes looking hurt and suspicious of the crowded world into which he had so unceremoniously been dumped. Tom was an entirely new personality, for whom his mother had hitherto been simply a convenient means of transport and sustenance. Laura would have to get to know this new personality.

With the love for her baby came a new confidence. The birth had finally laid the ghost of her upbringing. Laura Fisher was a complete person. Not only had she overcome the traumas to rebuild her own personality, she was also capable of creating new life. The mould was broken. The past was utterly vanquished; now she could look forward to the future.

This flood of love came so unexpectedly that Laura was briefly tempted towards sentimentality. Maybe she should put her career on hold, take a few years out and be a full-time Mum until Tom went to nursery school . . . ? For a moment she even contemplated rescinding her decision not to breastfeed him.

But the moment didn't last long. Laura Fisher knew she was strong enough to progress in her career and to look after Tom. On her own.

'Well, I must say I was *disappointed.*' Rob's lower lip jutted out in a comical *moue.* 'I thought I was your *friend* and when I ask if there's anything I can do to help, you don't say, "Yes, I'm in labour — rush me to hospital." No, it's just — "Get me a cab, could you, love?" I feel positively *passed over.*'

'I didn't want Dennis to know what was happening. I couldn't have tolerated all the inevitable lines about bloody women not being able to finish anything because they're always rushing off to have bloody babies.'

'All right, I'll forgive you.' But Rob didn't sound fully appeased.

'How is the old bastard, anyway?'

'As grotesque and charmless as ever. Still, he did actually sign your card from the production team, so aren't you the lucky one?'

'Hm.'

'Editorial meetings the last two mornings have

been dire — but *dire*. Really crappy ideas coming up. Dennis's been effing and blinding and stamping his little foot, because — say what you like about him — he can always recognize shit when he sees it. Takes one to know one, you could say. No, you've only been away for two programmes and already he's missing your inestimable contribution.'

'Good,' said Laura.

In his perspex cot at the side of her bed, Tom stirred under his much-washed blue cotton blanket. Laura, as recommended by the hospital for first-time mothers, would be staying in for nearly a week. Her initial reaction on hearing the suggestion had been to disagree and contemplate discharging herself after forty-eight hours. But reason had prevailed. There would be no one to help her when she got back to the flat and, besides, she needed to build up her strength before she took over the full responsibility of looking after Tom.

He was making the little hacking noise which Laura now recognized preceded crying, and she heaved herself up on the pillows. 'Pass him to me, would you, Rob?'

'Really?'

'Well, don't look so surprised. I'm sure you can manage to pick a baby up. He's not very heavy.'

'No. It's just . . . some people wouldn't like the idea of my handling their baby.'

It took Laura a second or two to realize what

he meant. 'Oh, for God's sake, Rob! Surely you've known me long enough to know I wouldn't think that. What, so I'm meant to be afraid homosexuality's so infectious that Tom'll catch it just being touched by you . . . ?'

Rob looked embarrassed. 'There are people who think like that.'

'There are people who want to bring back hanging, but I'm not one of them. Go on, pick him up.'

'Yes.' He moved awkwardly towards the cot. 'Not something I've done before.'

'There's no problem about it. Just make sure you support his head.'

With infinite care, and rather touching anxiety, Rob picked the tiny bundle out of its cot and passed it to Laura. The movement quieted Tom's crying. Rob looked down at the little face. 'Rotten, really, never to have one of these. Never to have the prospect even. Sometimes regret my sex life is entirely recreational. Procreational bit must be very exciting.'

Realizing that he was transgressing the rules of flippancy that governed their relationship, he added, 'Not of course that I'm saying the recreational bit isn't *good*. Dear oh dear, *so* good, so *very* good. Maybe you should try it with another woman, Laura . . . ? Maybe that's what's been wrong with your sex life all these years.'

As Tom leeched on to the teat of the bottle she offered him, Laura asked mildly, 'What makes you think there has been anything wrong with my sex life?'

'Simply that it doesn't seem to be terribly *active.*'

She too took refuge in flippancy. 'Pretty unusual to be very active in the week after you've given birth.'

'Yes, but I mean generally . . . Considering how attractive you are, it's amazing how few boyfriends you've had.'

'I am still technically married.'

'Yes, but . . .'

'Maybe I'm just too picky,' she said lightly. 'Maybe now I've tried living on my own for a while, I realize how little I need a man around cluttering up my space.'

'Hm, maybe that's it. And probably it's an absolutely *ideal* situation . . . so long as you can do without sex for long periods.'

'You have no idea how long I go without sex. You know nothing about my sex life, Rob.'

'No . . .' he agreed, 'except I definitely know that you had a bit nine months ago . . .'

If this had been a cue to confess the identity of Tom's father, Laura ignored it. 'Certainly did,' she said, shifting the baby in her arms and removing the bottle as he let out a little choking sound. She sat the floppy body up and patted its tiny rounded back. Tom let out a little cough and a posset of milk slipped down his chin. Laura wiped it with a muslin nappy and resettled him with the bottle in his mouth.

'Rob . . .' she began slowly. 'There *is* something I'd like you to do for me now . . .'

'Yes. Anything, my love. Anything you ask.' A sudden thought gave him pause. Raising his hands to his face in a gesture of mock-panic, he shrieked, 'Oh my *God!* You don't want me to change his nappy, do you?'

Tom stirred uneasily at the noise. 'Ssh,' said Laura. 'No, Rob. What I want you to do is . . . I'm not religious . . . I probably won't ever have Tom christened, but nonetheless . . . I'd really like it if you'd agree to be a kind of godfather for him.'

Rob's hands flickered up to his face again in a parody of Miss World-winning surprise. '*Moi?*'

'*Oui. Toi.*'

'Oh, but come *on.* I thought godparents were meant to take on the moral guardianship of their charges, point them in the way of the Lord and all that. I'm honestly not sure that I'm qualified.'

'Seem perfectly qualified to me.'

'But don't godfathers also take their godsons off to brothels to get them sexually initiated . . . or have I got that wrong? I mean, just *imagine* what kind of sexual practices I might initiate young Tom into.'

Laura was not put off. 'Please. I want you to agree to do it.'

Rob fluttered his eyelashes and again escaped into facetiousness. 'Well, if I say yes straight away, you're going to think I'm *easy,* aren't you?'

'No. Go on. Please will you? Please, be Tom's unofficial godfather.'

For a moment he mimed indecision, then conceded, 'All right, you've talked me into it.'

And Laura could see from his face how much her request had meant to him.

'Don't you want to hold him?' asked Laura.

'No.' Kent sat on a metal-framed hospital chair, the rigidity of his body signalling his unease. He looked more rectangular than ever in a dark grey suit. His hands clasped a rolled-up *Evening Standard* between his knees. The dull eyes were wrinkled about with exhaustion.

'But you must get to know him, Kent. There's no way you're going to avoid seeing a lot of him in the future, so you'd better come to terms with that.'

'What do you mean — see a lot of him?'

'Well, he's part of me now. If you see me, you'll see Tom. You know, on family occasions.' Kent let out a little grunt of annoyance. 'What's the matter?'

'It's just to hear you talk of "family occasions" . . . as if it were normal . . . as if we were part of a normal family that could have "family occasions".'

'Kent . . .' She wanted to reach out and touch him, pass on her new serenity, stroke his arm, melt away some of the tension inside. But touching didn't come within the agreement of their relationship. 'Kent, don't you understand, that was all in the past. It really is possible to put the whole business behind us. Now that he . . . our father's dead.' It annoyed her that she still stumbled on mentioning their father's name. 'We really can change, Kent. Tom's part of that change for me. He's going to grow up surrounded by love, I'll see to that. It really will be different for Tom.'

Her brother made no response. 'If only I could make you understand, Kent, how different *I* feel now I've got him. Cleansed almost, as though my childhood really has been purged away. It could work for you too. If you met someone you liked, if you just trusted yourself, then you could start a family and —'

'Shut up!' he said, surprisingly harsh. Then, covering the lapse, he went on, 'I'm sorry. I'm tired.'

'But it could work for you.'

'No. We've been through this many times. All right, I'm prepared to believe it's the right thing for you, Laura. I just know it isn't for me.'

'But why?'

'Because . . . I feel it's still in me . . . the capacity for violence is still . . .'

Laura tried to help as his words trickled away. 'You mean — "bad blood will out"?'

'If you like. Patterns repeat themselves.'

'But don't you see? You dilute the bad blood. You start afresh.' She indicated Tom, nuzzled sleepily content against her breast. 'I mean, look at him. Can you see any evil in that? He's starting afresh. He has the potential to become anything, everything.'

The seriousness of their conversation was unsettling Kent. He didn't like getting into discussions of the past; he preferred their talk to remain uncontroversially bland or, if topics of that kind ran out, he favoured silence.

Kent rose to his feet and banged the rolled-up *Evening Standard* against his thigh. 'I'm sorry. I'm not very good company this evening.' This was an incongruous apology from someone who appeared never to have attempted to be good company. 'Had a hell of a few days.'

'Work?'

He nodded. 'Haven't been to bed for the last two nights. Our investigations were really getting close and then . . .' he sighed with exasperation '. . . it all got fucked up.'

'Can you tell me about it?'

'Don't see why not. The case is over — though not in the way any of us wanted it to be over.'

'What happened?'

Kent sank back on to his chair, drained of all energy. For once, he was prepared to talk about work, and doing so seemed to relax him. Laura comforted herself that preoccupation with an investigation probably explained her brother's lack of response to his nephew.

'You remember the Melanie Harris case? Strangling in a car park in Paddington — last October?' Laura nodded. 'Well, we'd been following up all kinds of leads, kept going cold, kept looking as if we'd never get anywhere on it.

'Then, suddenly, couple of weeks ago, we got something. Hot. Real definite proof of who we were after. Witnesses who'd seen him round the relevant place at the relevant time. We'd got a name at least — we knew who we were after. Been tracking him down for the last week . . . finally got him and pulled him in for questioning. We were so close and . . .' he sighed in exasperation '. . . now we'll never be able to prove it. We know it was him, but we'll never be able to prove it . . . so the case'll just be closed. God, it's so fucking annoying when you put in all the hard graft and don't get a result!'

'But why haven't you got a result? What happened?'

'Only bloody topped himself, didn't he?'

Kent unfurled his *Evening Standard* and spread it out on the bed so that an edge just touched Tom. Laura followed her brother's pointing finger. She was vaguely aware of a headline reading, 'MAN FOUND HANGED IN POLICE CELL', but it wasn't the words that grabbed her attention. It was the photograph. A head and shoulders studio portrait. Unmistakably of the man she had met in a bar the previous October. Tom's father.

PART TWO:
1993

ELEVEN

Laura Fisher pushed the greying hair back from her temple and tried to focus her mind on what the prospective parliamentary candidate was saying. The trouble was he had one of those voices, like a weatherman's or a financial analyst's, which discouraged attention. The words were clear, but delivered in such a way that their meaning soon got lost as the listener's mind glazed over. He was, in short, boring.

Still, it was because he was boring that he was in the Lewthwaite Studios that morning. He was paying to make himself less boring, and thus in theory to enhance his chances of selection as candidate by his local Conservative Association. Laura's private view was that it would take a total charisma transplant to make him suitable for any kind of public office, but it wasn't her job to say that. Her job was to encourage him to come back and pay for more training sessions. It was early days for the studios and every little helped.

Realizing that he had stopped talking, she put down the talkback key and said, 'Yes, there's something coming there, but it still sounds as though you're reading it.'

He was aggrieved. 'But I'm not reading it.'

'I know that. I know it's entirely spontaneous. What we've got to work on now is making it *sound* entirely spontaneous.' Before he could speak to defend himself, she rose from her upholstered swivel chair. 'I'll come through into the studio.'

The complex still smelt new, even though its conversion had been completed nearly five months before. Laura breathed a cocktail of paint, sawdust and freshly laid carpet as she pushed through the soundproof doors into the studio.

The building was a converted warehouse, formerly Lewthwaite & Sons, in St George's Road, within walking distance of Laura's house at the edge of Brandon Hill Park. Though the exterior of the studios remained shabby, inside everywhere looked good. The dominant colours were a kind of French navy and paler shades of blue, carried through from the walls to the tweedy upholstery of the easy-chairs and low sofas. Tables, shelves and surfaces were all painted matt black. 'No Smoking' stickers were much in evidence. Carefully chosen prints hung on the walls. Looking that good had not been cheap.

Nor had the equipment which was essential to give the studios any chance against the competition. There were plenty of other television and audio facilities round Bristol, and profit margins had to be tightly trimmed for Lewthwaite Studios to be in with a chance.

Staff were another expense. Andy the editor was the only full-timer, but others came and went according to bookings of the facilities. Fortunately there was no lack of freelancers around in Bristol, particularly since the BBC had cut their television commitment in the region.

The project had been funded fifty per cent from Laura and Rob's savings, twenty-five per cent from a second mortgage on her house, and topped up by a bank loan. The finances just about worked, so long as all the facilities were fully booked most of the time. But the recession in the television industry following the cynical Thatcherite distribution of ITV franchises meant that there were a lot of other set-ups offering production facilities at bargain basement prices.

Laura knew it would be tough — and Rob's illness didn't help — but she reckoned she would survive. She was prepared to be flexible and explore alternative uses for her studios. The four-day television production courses she'd organized had been encouragingly over-subscribed, bearing out the old truism that when there are no jobs, there's never any shortage of hopefuls willing to pay to train for them. The courses were a part of the business she intended to develop further.

She knew she was putting her own career on hold, but she also knew it made economic sense. Nobody was now commissioning the kind of large-scale documentaries for which she had made her name and won BAFTA awards. Maybe the climate would improve, but till it did, she was in with a much better chance than her many former colleagues in the industry who had no work and no prospects. Her prudence in financial matters had paid off. Though some friends had accused her of being pussyfooted, Laura Fisher had always known that the only possible basis for life as a single woman was unchallengable financial independence.

And the outgoings would diminish in time. Already she was finding having Tom at university cheaper than having him at boarding school. Everything else would get better too. For a long time Laura Fisher had trained her mind to exclude negative thoughts.

The prospective parliamentary candidate looked up pathetically as she came into the studio. 'I wasn't reading it, really,' he protested.

'I know you weren't, but you still sounded as though you'd learnt it by heart.'

'Well, I had, I suppose, in a way. I mean, the statistics — you know, about what happened when we pulled out of the ERM — well, it wouldn't do if I got those wrong, would it?'

'No, obviously. But what you've got to do is make the things you've learnt off by heart sound as if you've just thought of them.'

'Oh.' He looked pessimistic. 'I don't think I'd be any good at that. I'm the sort of person who always does a lot of research and briefing before I go into a meeting or anything. I don't like presenting ideas as though I've just thought of them.'

'Sounding spontaneous needn't mean lacking authority. It's just that we live in the age of the sound-bite. Politicians have to be able to encapsulate their message in one, snappy sentence.'

He looked even more downcast. 'As I say, I don't think that sort of thing comes very naturally to me. Is it the kind of skill that can be learnt?'

'Of course it is,' Laura reassured him, knowing that in his case she was lying. 'And you must believe that too, or you wouldn't have booked in for this training, would you? Don't worry, we'll get there. It may take time, but we'll get there.'

She stole a look at her watch. Only twenty minutes gone of their two-hour session. God, this was uphill work. 'Tell you what,' she said, 'we'll try the same sort of straight-to-camera piece, but this time I'll put it on tape. Then we can go through it in detail . . . you'll be able to see when you're not sounding spontaneous . . . see where the body language looks wrong. OK?'

'OK,' said the prospective parliamentary candidate miserably.

She left the studios at one, politely deflecting the prospective parliamentary candidate's proposal of lunch. She had become adept over the years at turning down such offers. Though now pushing fifty, Laura Fisher was still a magnet for masculine attention. But she never offered any encouragement. If men became importunate, she fell back on the fiction of another lover, and was thus able to maintain her long habit of celibacy.

Andy was busy in the Online Edit Suite working on a corporate video. Laura gave him a wave through the small window in the door and noticed with satisfaction that the film's director was accompanied by the client who had commissioned the work. The client had seemed a nitpicker, likely to argue with the director over every edit, which meant the session would probably overrun, which in turn meant more money for Lewthwaite Studios. Laura didn't like to find herself thinking in such a mercenary way, but circumstances made it unavoidable.

She was going to work at home that afternoon, sorting through her old files to devise a course on the making of television documentaries. It shouldn't be too difficult, and she had plenty of under-employed contacts in the business who would be more than willing to give the odd lecture for a hundred quid. Yes, then all she would need to do would be to sort out some clips from her old films, work out a four-day timetable and advertise in the trade press. Given the reaction to her other courses, she expected a large and prompt response to the offer. And she reckoned she could hike up the prices a bit on this one.

September was giving way gracefully to October. As she emerged into the pale, bright sunlight, and started the climb up to Brandon Hill Park, Laura once again approved her decision to move to Bristol. She had got out of London when Tom was five, unwilling to bring him up and send him to school in the capital. Bristol, with its excellent rail service, had proved an ideal base, and she quickly established an efficient sequence of mother's helps, capable of looking after her son when she was off working.

At thirteen he had gone away to boarding school. Now he was reading media studies, with the ultimate ambition of being a journalist, at the rather grandiosely named University of the West of England — what used to be called Bristol Poly — and was once again living at home.

All in all, Laura considered she had done well with Tom's upbringing. Her love for him had never wavered and, though the nature of her work had meant long absences, she hoped he had been aware of the continuity of that love. Her plans for his care while she was away had always been meticulous, and the right present would always have been there for a birthday or special celebration, even if she hadn't. The aim of Laura's life — to give her son an upbringing as different as humanly possible from her own — had been achieved.

In spite of her love for Tom, there was always a slight distance between them, a lack of intimacy that she sometimes regretted, but that she reckoned was the price all working mothers had to pay. She had juggled the demands of family and career with skill and compassion.

Tom had grown up a quiet, reserved boy, but those were qualities that Laura could recognize in herself and did not worry her. He did not seem to have many friends, but then she had always held back from giving too much of herself to others. It was difficult to tell what he was thinking for much of the time, but Laura could empathize with a reticence which matched her own.

At times this reticence bordered on the secretive. He would sometimes disappear without explanation for days on end. Laura did not quiz him about these absences. He was nineteen, after all, and she hoped they meant he was quietly developing his own social life.

She loved him, of that she had never had any doubt. And she felt fairly confident that Tom loved her, though it would not have been in his nature to put the sentiment into words. She sometimes wished that she had produced a more confident, outgoing child, but had come to terms with the fact that Tom had inherited the quietness of her own personality. At least he had shown no signs of the murderous nature shared by his grandfather and father. If he had a fault, it lay in the repression of anger and violence; his inability to express adversarial feelings at times clearly caused him mental pain.

When she first discovered the identity of the man who had impregnated her, Laura had been thrown into turmoil. She had spent many sleepless nights, agonized by Kent's words about bad blood and patterns repeating themselves, but gradually the panics had faded. What erased them was Tom himself, his beauty, his charm. It was impossible to believe the existence of congenital evil in such a perfect shape.

By the time they moved to Bristol, the anxiety

had vanished completely. Five-year-old Tom, with his ash-blond hair and surprisingly blue eyes, had to be on the side of the angels. The circle of evil had been broken. Laura's decision to have a child on her own had been vindicated.

That did not mean of course that Tom was perfect. Throughout his life he had many habits that annoyed his mother. His passivity was the one that surfaced when she returned that afternoon to their neat house in Charlotte Street South. Tom lolled on the sitting room sofa, with the television on and the remote control drooping loosely in his hand.

'What are you watching?'

'I don't know.'

The answer was predictable and always stimulated a little spurt of anger in Laura. As someone who had spent all her professional life in television, she hated the zapping mentality of the younger generation. Programmes were made by programme-makers. Bad ones should be ignored, good ones should be sought out and watched with reverence. The idea of flicking randomly from channel to channel was anathema to Laura.

'Have you done anything about lunch?' she asked, knowing the answer to that question would be equally predictable.

'No. I wasn't sure when you were coming back. I didn't want to start doing anything in case you'd got something planned.'

'I hadn't got anything planned . . .' Laura stomped through to the kitchen '. . . beyond making some toast and putting some tarama, pâté and cheese out on a tray . . .'

'Fine then.' Tom pressed the remote control to change channel yet again.

'Something which I would have thought you were quite capable of doing for yourself!' Laura shouted through the kitchen door.

'Oh, it's all right, Mum. Chill out.'

'Well, it's easy enough for you to . . .' Laura restrained herself and was silent. She didn't want to degenerate into the parody of a nagging parent, but she had to admit that living with Tom was not as easy as she had expected it to be. They hadn't spent so much time together for a long time — since before he had started boarding in fact. During his school holidays they had either gone away together or Laura had been off working. Now, while she developed Lewthwaite Studios, she was spending much more time at home than she was used to.

She had discouraged Tom from going to university in Bristol. She thought he ought to show more enterprise and look further afield. But he had been adamant. The media studies course fitted his ambitions, and he seemed to like the idea of living with his mother. 'Give us a chance to get to know each other,' he had once said with one of his enigmatic, half-humorous smiles.

'We know each other perfectly well,' she had countered.

'Oh yes?'

It distressed Laura that Tom aggravated her

so much. Perhaps she just wasn't used to living with someone else in the house so much of the time. She also had an unworthy suspicion that Tom's desire to live at home was a kind of cowardice, a fear of venturing into the outside world. It riled her to think that she hadn't brought up a child whose independence of spirit matched her own.

Another factor in her dissatisfaction was the distrust of college training instinctive to someone who had learnt their craft the hard way. Laura had become a producer of television documentaries by working in the medium, moving from researcher to *Newsviews* feature director to ever bigger projects. She had genuine doubts whether anyone could learn journalism from sitting in a lecture hall. If Tom really wanted to work on newspapers, he should go out and work on newspapers.

She looked at her son as she brought the tray of lunch in from the kitchen. The sofa seemed too low for him and his legs took up a disproportionate amount of the carpet. The ash-blond hair which had made him such a stunning five-year-old had long ago dulled to light brown. It looked to her as if it could do with a wash, but she knew better than to raise the subject. The brilliant blue eyes seemed also to have dulled and taken on a slight shiftiness as he grew older. Spots burgeoned between Tom's eyebrows and gathered beneath the corners of his mouth.

Laura felt an unreasoning regret that he didn't

look better. Why couldn't she have produced a son who had outgrown the symptoms of adolescence by the time he was nineteen? Why couldn't she have had more control over the way Tom had turned out?

He zapped the remote once again, and Laura felt certain he had done it to annoy her. Whether he had or not, she snapped, 'Switch it off unless you're actually watching something.'

With a sigh of long-suffering at the unreasonableness of all parents, Tom switched the television off.

'Didn't you have any lectures this morning?'

'No.'

'Been working at home?'

'Done a bit.'

Laura didn't know whether to believe him or not. She knew she must stop imposing her own energy and imperatives on to her son, but sometimes it was hard. She tried to reason that she was almost a workaholic, and Tom's laid-back approach was a lot healthier, but she only half-convinced herself.

'Going in this afternoon?' she asked, hoping the enquiry sounded casual rather than reproachful.

From Tom's sigh it clearly hadn't been casual enough. 'May do. Probably. Got some research I should be doing in the library.'

'Research on what?'

But this was a question too far. Tom clammed up again and replied, 'Oh, this and that.'

Laura knew she shouldn't, but couldn't help continuing her catechism. 'Going to be out this evening?'

'No. Don't think so.'

'I thought students were meant to have a wild social life.'

'So?'

'Well, you don't seem to.'

'I see the people I want to see.'

'When? I don't see much evidence of you seeing them.'

'I see them when I want to see them,' he replied gnomically and unhelpfully.

Laura forced herself into silence. She didn't consider that she nagged, but she knew that's how it might appear to an outsider. That was also, so far as she could tell, how it appeared to Tom. Rob's view was that Laura's personality, her relentless efficiency, had frightened Tom off. He didn't want to enter any kind of competition with his mother, for fear that he might lose. In effect, what Rob was saying was that Laura swamped her son.

Occasionally she worried there might be an element of truth in the theory. Thinking about Rob brought his illness back into her mind. Things weren't looking too good. She didn't dare contemplate what would happen to their partnership and the finances of Lewthwaite Studios if he were to die. Must go and visit him again soon, she reminded herself.

'Oh,' said Tom suddenly, a half-eaten slice of

toast and taramasalata in his hand. 'A bloke came round this morning looking for you.'

'Bloke? What bloke?'

Tom seemed deliberately to evade her direct question. 'I said you'd be in this afternoon. He said he'd call then.'

'Who was he? What was his name?'

'Said his name was Michael Rowntree,' Tom replied casually.

TWELVE

If he hadn't given his name, she wouldn't have recognized him. Michael's hair had virtually all gone, only a few wisps were left, tucked away behind his ears. And whereas, when she had last seen him he had been running to fat, he was now cadaverously thin. He could have been in his sixties rather than his fifties.

His clothes were filthy — a checked shirt whose frayed collar was rimmed with grime, trousers of beige corduroy here and there worn smooth, a sports jacket whose tweed was dimmed with dirt and some of whose seams had unravelled. On his feet were grubby blue trainers with white flashes. His body gave off a sour odour. He looked like one of the homeless whom the recession had driven on to the streets of Britain's cities.

More disturbing than Michael's physical decrepitude, however, was his expression. His eyes had the unfixed glaze of insanity. Laura was glad that Tom hadn't yet left for college. He was upstairs, supposedly 'getting library stuff together'.

'Aren't you going to invite me in then?' asked Michael.

She had not been intending to, but somehow this direct question was impossible to refuse. He came through into the sitting room. 'Very nice,' he said, looking round. 'Very nicely done.'

'Would you like coffee or tea?'

'Coffee would be very nice, thank you.' This formality, still couched in public school vowels, came incongruously from his shabbiness.

Laura went through into the kitchen to make the coffee. She kept half a nervous eye on the sitting room, where Michael paced uneasily. He made her feel she would have to count the silver after he had gone.

While she ground the beans and filled the cafetière, Laura scoured her mind for the last she had heard of her former husband. There had been some professional falling out soon after their divorce, and Michael had left the family firm to start his own estate agency. That had presumably suffered in the property collapse of the late eighties. She remembered hearing from a mutual acquaintance that Michael had financial problems.

He had also remarried, she had heard, but something had gone wrong there too. Michael had suffered the fate of many who thought the world owed them a living and found out too late that the world wasn't aware of any such obligation. So Laura had expected him to be in reduced circumstances, but she was nevertheless shocked at how reduced those circumstances were.

When she came back in with the coffee tray, he was looking at the photographs on her mantelpiece. They formed a little gallery of Tom's development, from blond toddler to self-effacing adolescent. For the past six years he had refused to be photographed.

'So this is the "love child", is it?' Michael sneered.

'That's Tom. You saw him this morning,' Laura replied crisply, and sat down to pour the coffee. 'Why have you come here, Michael? What do you want?'

'Just to see you.' He gave an ingenuous shrug. 'Does there have to be a reason? Isn't it better that we should remain good friends?'

'We never were particularly good friends, Michael. And, in reply to your question, I would say there does have to be a reason for you to come to visit me so suddenly. It's over fifteen years since we last saw each other.'

An unnerving smugness came into his face. 'It's over fifteen years since *you* last saw *me*.'

'What do you mean by that?'

'I've seen you a good few times, Laura.'

'Where?'

'Here . . . there . . . and everywhere . . . as the Beatles so inimitably put it.' He gave a little self-congratulatory chuckle. 'I've kept an eye on you, Laura. I'll always keep an eye on you.'

'I don't believe it.' But even as she dismissed the idea, she did believe it. The feeling that Michael was spying on her had never quite gone away. She had argued with herself that it was ridiculous, that she hadn't really seen him turning away from her gaze in a crowd from time to time, but his words now refuelled the old anxiety.

He didn't elaborate, but sat looking at her, a complacent smile on his face. He was behaving as though he had some kind of control over her, though Laura could not imagine what it might be.

'I go back to my question, Michael. Why have you come here?'

'I need some help. I thought you could help me.'

'What kind of help?'

'Financial help.'

'Hm. Well, putting aside for one moment the issue of whether I would want to give you any financial help, I must also tell you you've come at a bad time. I've put all my savings into equipping my own studios. Not a lot of cash-flow around at the moment.'

'I only need five hundred. Just to tide me over.'

'I haven't got five hundred to spare. And if I did have, I could think of more deserving causes.'

He was sullenly aggrieved by this response. 'Don't be hasty, Laura. You might come to regret a hasty decision.'

'In what way would I regret it?'

'I have certain information about your past, which you might not wish to reach the ears of . . . certain people.'

'Are you threatening me?'

'Yes.'

She didn't feel threatened. Michael didn't know the identity of Tom's father, so the only information he had which he might think damaging was the fact that Richard Fisher had murdered his wife. And, though Laura didn't regularly volunteer that in conversation, she never denied it if someone else raised the subject.

Also, who on earth did Michael mean by 'certain people'? Laura ran her own business and was answerable to no one. The idea that he could blackmail her by snitching to an employer showed how hopelessly out of touch he was with the real world. That was actually much more worrying than the content of his threats. He seemed increasingly unhinged. In his eye was the wildness that would make people hurry away from him in the streets. Once again she was glad that Tom was still in the house.

'I don't know what you're talking about, Michael,' she said in a level tone. 'There's nothing you can tell anyone about me that could do any harm.'

'I could tell them about what happened on our wedding night.'

This was unbelievable. His mind had clearly gone. 'Tell who, Michael? Who might possibly be interested in what happened on our wedding night? If one of us was a soap star or minor royal, maybe . . . Anyway, I would have thought what happened on our wedding night reflected badly on you rather than on me.'

'Yes, but . . . There are other things I could tell . . .' His eyes went dreamy as he lost concentration and it was with a struggle that he brought himself back to the subject. When he did, he was almost incoherent. Laura wondered whether he was on drugs.

'Lots of things I could tell, Laura . . . Things about violence . . . murder . . . There are things in your past that could destroy you, Laura . . . I could destroy you, Laura. I could still destroy you. After the way you behaved to me . . . there's a debt to be paid . . .'

If this was another threat, it was not delivered in a manner that was at all threatening. Michael seemed preoccupied, his words dragged out of some deep reverie.

Laura decided it was time to get rid of him. 'I'm sorry, I should be working. I must ask you to leave, Michael.' Against her better judgement, she took out her cheque book and gave him a hundred pounds. 'And that's more than I can afford. So take it and don't come back. There won't be any more, I promise you that.'

'Aren't you going to ask me where I'm living, what I'm doing with my life?' he asked, in a manner that was perhaps meant to be boyishly appealing.

'No, Michael. I'm not interested.'

He stood up, and once again looked round her sitting room. There was something she didn't like about his proprietorial manner. Her possessions seemed tarnished by his stare.

'I'd appreciate it if you'd leave, Michael.'

'All right, all right. I'm going. No need to be offensive.' He folded her cheque and shoved it into his jacket pocket, but made no move towards the door.

'Please,' Laura said firmly. 'I don't want to have to call anyone to get rid of you.'

'Call anyone? Call the police, do you mean? Call brother Kent? Still see him, do you?'

'Yes.'

'Still protecting you like the faithful Rottweiler, is he? Live down here, does he?'

'Kent's now a Detective Inspector based in Bristol.'

'Oh, I see. Still can't keep away from you, can he? Joined at the bloody hip, you two, aren't you? Joined by the violence that your —'

'Shut up, Michael!' It wasn't that his words hurt; she just wanted him to go. Laura moved into the hall and opened the front door. Behind her she heard movement on the stairs. Tom, drawn by her shouting, peered curiously down into the hall. He carried his college bag.

Michael looked up at the boy and smiled sardonically. 'We meet again.'

'Yes.'

'You look after your mother, do you, Tom?'

The boy gave a non-committal shrug.

'Very well protected, aren't you, Laura? Tom on the spot, Kent here in Bristol too. I suppose you think you've got enough protection, don't you?'

'Goodbye, Michael,' said Laura pointedly, her hand on the door handle.

'Well, you're going to need all the bloody protection you can get!' With sudden savagery, Michael strode across the hall and left, shutting the front door behind him. The house shuddered with the impact. Laura nursed her wrist, wrenched by the slamming door.

There was an enigmatic half-smile on Tom's face. 'So . . . that was Michael Rowntree, your former husband?'

'Yes.'

'But not my father.'

'No. Tom, if ever you do want to talk about —'

'Must go. Got to get to the library. Research, research, research, that's what busy little journalism students do.' He bustled past her, blowing a parodic kiss. 'See you later, "Mummy".' And he was gone.

When he called her 'Mummy', Tom was always being ironic. Once again Laura wondered how interested he really was in his father's identity. For nineteen years Tom had shown a studied lack of curiosity on the subject, and yet he would not be human if he didn't wonder about it from time to time. Occasionally he would hint at the mystery, as he just had done with his words, 'But not my father.' Once it had been aired, though, he would always move swiftly on, as he had just demonstrated.

Laura herself had tried to raise the subject on numerous occasions. She didn't have a crusading conviction that Tom ought to know the truth; she just felt he should have the option of knowing it if he wanted to. So far, except for the odd teasing reference like the one he'd just made, the boy had shown no sign of wanting to.

And Laura couldn't help admitting that his lack of curiosity suited her very well. The man, when she had picked him up in the bar, had been irrelevant, merely a means to an end. And in Laura Fisher's mind, he was still irrelevant.

'Michael came round today.'

'Oh?' Kent's voice at the other end of the line was instantly alert. 'Was he all right? He didn't give you any trouble?'

'Not exactly. He was very strange. He doesn't seem quite right in the head.'

'No. He isn't.'

'How do you know?'

'He's been in trouble with the police more than once over the last few years. Been in prison twice.'

'Really? What kind of trouble was it? What was he in for?'

'He beat up a couple of women.'

Laura felt a little chill at these words. How would the afternoon's scene have ended if Tom had not been there?

'Don't worry,' Kent went on, solid and reassuring as ever. 'I'll keep an eye on him.'

'Just like you keep an eye on me . . . ?'

'Yes,' he replied in a voice totally without emotion. 'Are you still on for this evening?'

'Sure,' she said, '. . . if it's all right with Viv.'

'It's all right with Viv,' Kent replied.

THIRTEEN

Laura had been very surprised when Kent announced he was getting married. Surprised, but relieved. It had been soon after he was transferred to Bristol, which had been within a year of her moving down there. Initially she had been worried that he had sought the relocation because of her, to continue the protection which he had always provided. But he had later told her he had moved because of Viv. She was a WPC he had met in London, and when she got a job in Bristol he had followed.

The idea of her brother marrying had always seemed so remote that Laura supposed Viv was no less likely a bride for him than anyone else. She was a few years older, forty to his thirty-six when they married. It was second time around for her; she had a twenty-year-old daughter, Denise, from her marriage to a man she habitually referred to as 'the piece of piss'.

Viv was always raucous and vulgar. Laura could not suppress the knowledge that her murdered mother would have classified her as 'common'. A tall, spare woman with short black hair now streaked with grey, Viv uttered her customary string of obscenities in a voice which had the incisive rasp of a chain-smoker. She fitted well into the blokish world of the police force, giving as good as she got in coarse exchanges with her male colleagues. Her conversation was scatological and she was always talking about sex.

Laura assumed that sex was the basis of her relationship with Kent. On the comparatively rare occasions when they were seen in company they did not appear to have a lot in common, he stiff and taciturn as ever, Viv noisy and extrovert. But perhaps her crude lack of sentimentality struck a chord with Kent's deep cynicism. Perhaps he got turned on by her talking dirty.

It wasn't entirely a traditional marriage. Their shift patterns meant at times they saw little of each other. Kent early on had expressed a dislike of foreign holidays, so Viv and Denise would go off abroad on their own while he booked in for courses in such vigorous pursuits as rock climbing or scuba diving.

There had never been any thought of their having children. Viv began many sentences with the words, 'If you think I'm going through all that bloody business again . . .' 'No,' she would go on, 'I love Denise very much, but she's the only one I want, thank you very much.'

And whenever her mother said this, Denise would giggle as at some private joke. She was a colourless girl, almost white-blond hair and pale blue eyes with lashes like wood-shavings. Whenever anyone commented on her lack of likeness to her mother, Viv would say, 'No, takes after the piece of piss, poor little brat,' before bursting into raucous laughter.

A little titter from Denise would echo this. The girl was meek and self-effacing, as quiet as Viv was noisy. She worked at a supermarket checkout and apparently had no ambition to move out of the three-bedroomed semi in Hotwells that her mother shared with her new husband. Denise seemed to have no identity of her own, content to be swept along by the wave of her mother's forceful personality.

Laura occasionally worried about the parallels between Kent's step-daughter and her own son. Was Rob right? Was Tom's passivity the natural corollary to her fierce will-power? But she comforted herself with the thought that Tom had nowhere near as pallid a personality as Denise. With him, Laura felt confident that the current apathy was only a stage, the tail-end of adolescence. Soon he would recapture the charm and energy of his earlier years and begin to assert his own identity.

Though they had become cousins by marriage, Tom and Denise were fifteen years apart in age. They had almost nothing in common and saw little of each other. As Kent had suggested when Tom was born, there were very few 'family occasions'. In spite of the changes in their circumstances, Laura and Kent did not belong to that kind of family.

However unlikely Kent's pairing with Viv might look to an outsider, the marriage seemed to work. They stayed together, anyway, in their semi-detached way. There were no suggestions that either of them strayed from the marital bed, and no doubt their relationship was as unfathomably workable as most marriages. They were not particularly sociable, they certainly never made romantic gestures to each other in public, but like most married couples they jogged along.

For Laura, Kent's marriage had been an enormous relief. Not only did it still her fears about his never being able to form a liaison with a member of the opposite sex, it also diminished the claustrophobia of her relationship with her brother. Though she still appreciated his dour concern for her, she sometimes found his company a burden. With Kent, conversation could never lighten up; in his presence the shadow of their shared upbringing always loomed over them. At any moment he might bring the conversation back to the damage wrought on them by their father.

Whether he spilled out these gloomy thoughts to Viv or not — and somehow Laura thought it was unlikely — at least she herself had got less of them since he had married. Laura still saw a lot of her brother — if she was free Kent would take her out for dinner on Wednesday evenings, when Viv had a regular night shift — but their relationship seemed less intense and pressured.

Sometimes she saw the familiar bleak hopelessness in her brother's eyes, and with a slightly guilty relief convinced herself that it was no longer her problem. Marriage always weakens the intimacy between siblings, and the bond between Laura and Kent had never been so much an intimacy as a shared trauma.

Laura and Viv were never going to be soul-mates, but they each respected the other's value to Kent. Viv never made any demur about him spending so much time with his sister, but equally did not volunteer to join them. The two women were not close, though pleasant enough to each other on the rare occasions when they did meet. Each had keys to the other's house and helped with domestic chores like watering plants during holidays. That kind of service — being of use to someone without actually meeting them — seemed an ideal form of communication between two women with so little in common.

Very occasionally Laura, Kent and Viv met up as a threesome — well, foursome actually, because Denise almost always tagged wanly along. Tom never joined them.

These evenings were rarely in their homes. Although they lived relatively close and Kent would frequently come on his own to Laura's house, she almost never went to his. Viv clearly felt ill at ease amidst the middle-class gentility of her sister-in-law's surroundings, and she 'was buggered if she was going to cook some crap meal at home when there was a perfectly good Tandoori just round the corner'. So they always went out to eat.

Laura never found these evenings relaxing. Viv drank too much and got noisier; Denise drank too much and got gigglier; Kent drank too much and got increasingly silent. It was always a relief to get back to the calm of the house in Charlotte Street South. But dinner at the Tandoori was a ritual that had to be gone through two or three times a year, the nearest the Fishers would ever get to a 'family occasion', when four people would spend an evening together trying to pretend they had something in common.

The evening after Kent's call was no different from any of the others. They went of course to the Tandoori. The conversation was jerky until alcohol made it more fluent. Kent and Viv drank lager, Laura and Denise white wine.

'How's that Tom of yours?' asked Viv through a mouthful of curry.

'He's fine.'

'Any girlfriends yet?'

'Not that I know of.'

'Working too bloody hard to have a sex life, eh?' Viv suggested slyly. 'Like his mother . . . ?'

Laura let the gibe go unchallenged. She was certainly not going to give any confidences to her sister-in-law. Viv opened her mouth and blew out, fanning her face with her hand. The curry had brought a film of sweat to her nose and cheeks.

'Important when you're young,' she went on, 'to know what kind of sex you want and to go out and bloody get it.' She erupted into a laugh. 'Not just when you're young either.'

'Sometimes you don't meet the right person,' said Laura casually.

'Then you're not bloody looking hard enough! I've always known what I wanted — and I've gone out and got it.' Denise tittered as Viv looked across at her husband. 'Haven't I, Kent?'

He nodded awkwardly, embarrassed. 'Oh yes.'

'That's what you've got to do — know what you bloody want and go out and get it,' Viv repeated. She took a long swallow of lager to cool her down, then grinned at her daughter. 'That's what you do, don't you, Denise?'

The girl giggled again. 'Oh yes. I get what I want.'

It seemed strange to Laura to think of this mouse having any kind of sex life, but the knowing wink to her mother implied Denise knew what she was talking about. The girl was nearly thirty-five, after all, and in spite of her self-effacement, did not seem to lack confidence. No doubt she could find men when she wanted to.

Laura felt a momentary pang of jealousy for the idea of normal sexual development, growing up with the opposite sex, experimenting, having good experiences and bad, feeling that sexuality was normal. But it soon passed. She had done all right. Tom was her achievement. Tom and her career. And balancing the demands of both. There should be no higher human ambition than to bring up a child surrounded by love.

'Tell you what,' said Viv, wiping her mouth with the back of her hand after a long draught

149

of lager, 'I really fancy a bit of sex tonight.' She looked up at the waiter who had just arrived to deliver some extra poppadoms they had ordered. 'Said I fancied a bit of sex tonight.'

The waiter smiled nervously and Viv guffawed as he moved apologetically away. Denise snickered a little laugh. Her mother grinned and repeated, 'No, really fancy a bit . . .' She looked across at Kent '. . . if that's all right with you, husband dear . . . ?'

'Oh yes, that's all right with me.'

As he said the words, Kent looked at his sister, and there was a kind of schoolboy defiance in his eyes, as if to say, 'There — be shocked if you want to.'

Laura didn't want to. The exchange had not shocked her, just revived her surprise at the way Kent's life had turned out. Viv was so overt, so up-front, so . . . no, the word 'common' could not be avoided . . . and yet there was no doubt she was exactly what Kent needed.

Never mind, thought Laura. It would have been an undeserved bonus for him to have married someone whom I felt to be a soul-mate. The growing gulf between brother and sister was a small price to pay if it offered Kent some hope of happiness.

FOURTEEN

'This is Emily.'

The girl was about Tom's age, with pale blue eyes and dark brown hair, centre-parted and hanging loose on to her shoulders. She was pretty in a sort of sixties-revival way. A little cluster of silver hung from one pierced ear. She wore the student uniform of heavy boots, black Levis and a grey sweatshirt a few sizes too big. Its sleeves dangled long and she seemed to have pulled them longer to make them cover her hands. This gave her a waiflike appearance, and Laura felt sure the effect was deliberate.

It was strange how instinctive her distrust — or even dislike — of the girl was. Laura tried to control the reaction. God knew, she had wished enough times for Tom to find a girlfriend, and now he'd done so she was immediately finding fault. She wondered if it was just her maternal hackles rising at any threat to the exclusivity of her relationship with her son, but quickly decided it wasn't. There was something about Emily, a kind of serene smugness, that positively antagonized Laura. The proprietorial way the girl looked at Tom seemed calculated, a cocky challenge to his mother.

But Tom had at last brought a girlfriend home,

and that had to be good news. It was also a mild surprise. Rob always joked heavily about his 'godson' being gay, saying how much fun he would have as soon as he came clean and recognized the fact. Tom never failed to be deeply embarrassed by such talk, but he liked Rob and, though hotly denying the allegation, submitted to the joshing with good humour.

While Laura didn't really believe that her son was gay, something of Rob's insinuation rubbed off on her and she wouldn't have been totally surprised to discover it was true. The presence of Emily at least seemed to put paid to that speculation.

Anyway, whatever her instinctive antipathy to the girl, Laura knew that the appropriate courtesies had to be exchanged. She extended her hand. 'Nice to meet you.'

Emily rolled back a sleeve and shook hands limply. 'And you.' When she withdrew her hand, the sleeve slipped down to cover it again. Her voice had a slight Welsh whine to it, which also, unreasonably, prejudiced Laura against her.

'Are you at the university too?'

A languid nod. 'Doing French and German.'

'Have you known each other long?' She addressed this question to Tom, but he, with an infuriating grin, deflected it, nodding towards Emily.

'Met at a disco couple of weeks back,' she drawled.

'I didn't know discos were your thing, Tom.'

'Lots you don't know about me, "Mummy".'

The girl's smugness was contagious. Laura didn't like the effect Emily was having on Tom, and she didn't like herself for not liking it. On the occasions when her imagination had supplied this scene, the girl her son brought home had been more open, more approachable, less sly than this real one.

'I thought we should meet up,' said Emily, 'now Tom and I are an "item".' The hands came out of their sleeves for the fingers to mime quotation marks round the word 'item'. It was a mannerism which Laura particularly disliked. 'Tom wasn't keen,' Emily went on, 'wanted to keep "us" a secret, but I thought it was best for you and me to meet.'

Tom looked sheepish, embarrassed at the way this young woman had taken over his will, but at the same time almost proud of his subjugation. He seemed to be watching Laura for her reaction, and she felt paradoxically that the reaction he wanted was disapproval. It was as if that would set the seal on the validity of his new relationship.

'Can I get you a drink or something, Emily?' asked Laura, over-compensating with charm for her real feelings.

'I don't drink alcohol.'

No, you bloody wouldn't. 'Tea then . . . or coffee?'

'Do you have any herbal tea?'

'No, I don't, actually.'

'Oh, well then, I won't bother, thanks.'

153

Laura picked up the bag put down when she had come in and been introduced to Emily. 'You will excuse me? I've got to get the train up to London — visit a friend in hospital . . .' She stopped herself from adding . . . 'and I thought Tom said he was going to come with me, but clearly he has *other plans* for the evening.'

To her surprise, though, Tom announced, 'Oh, we're coming too.'

'We?' Laura echoed.

'Mm. Emily and me.'

'Really?'

'To London. To see Rob.'

Laura evidently couldn't keep the amazement out of her face, because Emily felt called upon to explain, 'I think it's very important when you get to know someone to meet all the people around them. None of us exists in a vacuum simply as an individual; we're all made up of our reactions to the other people we know.'

Laura was rapidly coming round to the view that a little of Emily's pontificating might go a long way. She respected confidence in a woman, but she was riled by the girl's habit of making statements as though no alternative opinion was possible.

'Mm. Don't you think we should check with Rob? He's very ill. He may not feel up to meeting new people.'

'Be fine,' said Tom, picking up the casualness of Emily's tone. 'He keeps saying how boring we are whenever we go and see him, keeps saying

154

he's dying for "new blood".' He put a slight campness, an echo of Rob's manner, into the last two words.

What he said was true. Laura remembered Rob using that exact phrase.

'Besides, if there's any problem,' Emily interposed humbly, 'I don't mind just sitting in a waiting room or somewhere. I've got a book with me.'

'Fine,' said Laura through tight lips. 'I'll just go and get my coat and we'll be off.'

The journey to London did not raise Laura's opinion of her son's choice. Actually, the evidence seemed to build that he had been Emily's choice rather than the other way round. Tom, passive as ever, had just fallen in with her plans. Laura wondered yet again whether it was her own energy that had made her son so spineless.

There was no demur from either of them when Laura bought all the tickets. Though Emily had indeed got a book with her, unfortunately she did not read it. She preferred to talk.

It turned out on that journey that Emily was a feminist. This might perhaps have given her something in common with Laura, whose life had been a practical demonstration of one brand of feminism. But no, Emily's views made for greater distance rather than any rapprochement between them. Her version of feminism was predicated on 'political correctness', and seemed to Laura enmired in linguistics rather than having any application to real life.

Emily pontificated at length about the 'political incorrectness' of one of her lecturers, a Scot who insisted on referring to female students as 'wee girlies'. She said she had been forced to make a complaint about this to her tutor and then paused, as if expecting applause for her action.

She didn't get any from Laura, who was becoming angrier and angrier. What annoyed her was not just the drivel that Emily kept spouting, but the rapt way in which Tom lapped it all up. She wouldn't have minded — or she told herself she wouldn't have minded — if she thought he was genuinely in love with the girl. Love, she knew, could sanctify for a time the most appalling personal characteristics. But the way Tom responded to Emily didn't look like love. His reaction seemed a mix of deference and eagerness to please. He certainly didn't seem relaxed with her.

'We're going to be very responsible about our relationship,' Emily suddenly announced after a merciful lull in her monologue.

'Ah,' said Laura, who had noticed that, unbelievably, they had still only got as far as Reading. 'Good.'

'Yes. We're going to get to know each other very well before we actually go to bed together.'

Tom turned scarlet and Laura felt an almost uncontrollable desire to giggle. 'Oh,' she said, 'you sweet old-fashioned things.'

'I'm not sure that it's very flattering,' Emily

reproved gently, 'to speak of us as "things". We are all people, you know.'

'Yes,' Laura agreed, 'yes. Aren't we just?'

'No, people go on about the younger generation having no sense of responsibility,' Emily ploughed on, 'but I think they misjudge us. We're certainly very concerned about issues like safe sex, aren't we, Tom?'

Surely he would try to wriggle out of the stranglehold of that "we", thought Laura. But no. Avoiding his mother's eye, he concurred with Emily's view.

'One interesting thing Tom said to me, Laura . . .'

'Mm.'

'He said he doesn't know who his father is.'

'No,' Laura agreed.

'Well, don't you think you ought to tell us?'

That 'us' nearly did make Laura lose her temper.

'Fuck it,' said Rob with exaggerated despair. 'I should have got bloody AIDS. That would at least have been a lifestyle statement. God knows, no one could have tried to get it harder than I did — had I known it existed, that is. And here I am dying of bloody lung cancer instead — how too, too *shame-making*.' He dropped into a Noel Coward parody for the last few words.

'You're not dying,' said Laura gently.

'Huh. Well, I feel like I'm dying. Honestly,' he went on, worrying away at the idea, 'lung cancer's so *common,* isn't it? I mean, everyone gets that. Even bloody Dennis Parker managed to die of lung cancer. I think AIDS has more dignity.'

'I'm not sure that many of the people dying of it would agree with you.'

'Well, from the outside it has more dignity. Looks more dignified to me.' A little cough shook his frail body. 'Not some crap disease contracted by any Tom, Dick and Harry who's capable of smoking sixty cigarettes a day. I'd mind less if I'd actually smoked myself. There's me, Mr Clean, being a good boy through all those endless studio days and meetings while everyone else was belching out smoke like Victorian Manchester . . . and I bloody get the disease too. Passive smoking, that's what they call it.' A thought struck him. 'I wonder if you can get passive AIDS if you're just a voyeur . . . ?' He looked straight at Laura. 'Didn't Tom come with you?'

'Yes, he's waiting outside. He's . . . got someone with him.'

'Oh?' Understanding dawned. Thin hands fluttered up to clasp his face in the old parody of surprise. 'Oh, wonderful! Oh, positively frabjous day! Calloo, callay! You mean he's got a boyfriend?'

'No. A girlfriend.'

'Aah.' The deep lines of his mouth dragged comically downwards. 'Well, there's a let-down. Has this been going on for long?'

'Pretty recent, I gather.'

'I'm sure it'll end in tears.'

'No, I don't think tears come into the scenario Emily has in mind.' Laura had tried to avoid saying anything judgemental about the girl, but knew from the sharp look in Rob's eye that she had failed.

'I see,' he said. 'Bit of a little madam, is she?'

'Well . . . Let's say she seems to be the one who's running the show.'

Rob gave her a teasing interrogative grin. Laura was tempted to say more. It would be very relaxing to slip back into one of their bitching sessions. But no, that wouldn't be fair. Rob hadn't even met the girl yet, for God's sake. She mustn't prejudice him against her.

Laura reproved herself for slipping so readily into the over-protective, no-woman's-good-enough-for-my-son stereotype of a mother. Perhaps her sourness was menopausal, she wondered. Seemed strange to think of that. She had always known it would come, seen it happen to friends and, in a detached way, she was aware now of it happening to her. It wasn't worrying, just seemed strange. She had that recurrent feeling of not being grown-up enough to be as old as she was.

She ignored the prompt in Rob's eye and said primly, 'There are a few decisions we've got to make about the studios. I think we should talk those through quickly before the others come in.'

'Spoil-sport.' Rob lay back in his bed, unable to get comfortable. He coughed again. 'Keep the character assassination until after I've met the little charmer, eh?'

There was no opportunity for the promised bitchery, since Laura, Tom and Emily all left the ward together. Laura reflected that this was probably just as well. Tempting though the prospect was, she must not pander to her worst instincts. And if Tom and Emily being an 'item' — in crook-fingered quotation marks — was going to become a fact of life, then it was one that Laura must come to terms with.

Rob's first comment on being introduced to Emily had been enigmatic. 'Your mother casts a long shadow, Tom,' he had said. In response to Laura's puzzled expression, he explained, 'I meant that you should be flattered.'

'Why?'

'Because Tom's chosen a girlfriend who looks so like you.'

'What!' Laura and Emily had spoken the word together, both equally affronted by the suggestion.

'I don't think we look anything alike,' said Laura.

'Nor do I,' Emily agreed hotly.

'Oh yes, there's definitely something about the colouring,' Rob insisted.

'No. My eyes are hazel and Emily's are blue.' Pale blue, Laura thought, very pale, very diluted blue. Almost as pale as Denise's.

'Still something about the contrast between the

dark hair and the light eyes. And the way you hold your heads. No, you look very like Laura did at your age, Emily.'

The girl's expression was dubious, not flattered by the comparison, but unwilling to be outright rude.

'Laura was an absolute stunner then,' Rob reassured. 'All the men on the *Newsviews* team were desperate to get inside her knickers. Not many succeeded, though, did they, Laura . . . ?'

She recognized this as another of Rob's periodic probes about the identity of Tom's father, but didn't respond to it. In spite of considerable pressure over the years, she had never told even Rob anything about the man. Laura Fisher was the only person in the world who knew that her son's father had been a murderer.

'Anyway, how're you feeling, Rob?' asked Tom, clumsily redirecting the conversation.

'Oh, you know, pretty good,' the emaciated figure in the bed replied with a bland grin. 'As good as you'd expect someone to feel when they're rotting away from the inside out.'

'There are great advances in the treatment of cancer these days,' said Emily seriously. 'Even lung cancer's no longer the death sentence it used to be.'

'Oh, thank you, dear. That's very comforting.'

Rob caught Laura's eye and she had to look away. There were a few other similar moments during the visit . . . like when Emily announced that she had no prejudice against people whose sexual orientation was different from her own . . . or whenever she referred to Tom as her 'partner'.

The first time this happened, Rob had asked ingenuously, 'Sorry, are you a firm of solicitors?' and Laura had had to convert her chortle into a cough.

Emily seemed not to notice that she was being sent up — or if she did, the knowledge didn't faze her. Laura realized that the girl was totally impervious to irony. Tom said little, apparently quite happy to pass over all conversational initiative to his girlfriend.

When the bell for the end of visiting sounded, everyone was quite relieved. As Laura kissed Rob goodbye, smelling the staleness of decay on his breath, he said, 'Do ring me tomorrow, *won't* you, Laura darling? I'm sure we'll have *so* much to talk about.' And, as she drew away, one of his sunken, exhausted eyes winked at her.

The prospect of her debriefing call to Rob the following day saw Laura through the interminable pontification of the journey back to Bristol.

FIFTEEN

Dear Laura,

I have thought many times about whether or not I should write to you, and will fully understand if you have no wish to make contact with me again after all this time.

As you will see from the address, I'm currently living in London. How long I will be staying here depends on a variety of factors.

To bring you up to date with my news . . . Two years ago, after a struggle that was very hard for me to bear, Julie died. My feelings about her are still very complex. I admired her enormously, we brought up two lovely children together, and in many ways it was a good marriage. Her death was a very draining experience for me, and perhaps I have blamed myself more than I should for betraying her with you, at first in reality, and since then many, many times in my imagination. If, as the Bible says, the guilt for adultery in the heart is as great as that for the real thing, I am still a very guilty man.

I'm sorry. Probably the last thing you want to read at the moment is the romantic maunderings of an old man in his late fifties. If so, just stop reading this letter now, throw it away, forget we ever met.

Practical details about my current life . . . Very soon after Julie's death I took — or was gracefully but firmly encouraged to take — early retirement from the company. I'd served my time all right and ended up as a kind of New Zealand guru of television documentaries. I could happily have filled my days giving lectures, doing workshops, talking at symposia and conferences for the rest of my life. And in the early months of my retirement I did quite a lot of that sort of thing. It was fine, but I still felt restless.

I started work on a long-term project which I've been nursing for some time, a kind of world history of broadcasting. I don't think such a book exists and I would like to leave behind something a bit less ephemeral than a television documentary. I did what research I could in Auckland, but obviously taking on such a massive subject I need to consult sources in other countries — in particular in America and England. But I kept dithering about what I should do — go for an extended trip abroad, pull up sticks completely, I didn't know. I ended up making the compromise I usually make, and did nothing. The world history of broadcasting was put on ice.

What polarized the intention to change my circumstances was Tammy remarrying. Her first marriage was a pretty total disaster — I won't bore you with the details, but sadly worries about it cast a cloud over Julie's last months. And I'm only sorry that she died before Tammy met her new man, who is everything the other wasn't. His name's Derek, they have a six-month-old baby called Katie and are deliriously happy.

But the main point is that Derek is a Brit. A cricket commentator, of all things. They met when he was over in New Zealand covering a Test series. So, although he still travels a lot, their base is now London. Since Paul and I have grown apart — again I won't go into details about all that — and since Tammy and I have remained very close through all the upheavals we've endured, there seemed a logic to my coming to London, at least to see how things worked out.

I've now been here eight months — I wanted to be in England for the birth of my first grandchild. I've been doing some quite useful research for my book in the British Library and the newspaper library at Colindale, but there hasn't been a day since I arrived when I haven't contemplated contacting you. Finally today, as you see, I have plucked up my courage and written this letter — with a kind of devil-may-care attitude that the worst you could say is 'No' — though that apparent insouciance is not an accurate reflection of my real feelings.

I'm sorry. I'm not finding this easy to write and I know I'm getting bogged down in syntax and parentheses. Basically, all I'm saying,

Laura, is that if you do want to see me again, please call me at the above number. I have no real expectations about what would happen if we did meet. I just feel that you and I once shared something which, certainly in my life, has never been matched or replaced. And it seems to me a pity that we should go to our graves without having at least seen each other again, to discover, I suppose, whether anything of what was once there remains. Though probably there won't be anything, but I'm sure we could at least still be polite to each other, if we met for lunch or something.

I'm not going to read this letter through. I know it's an incoherent mess, and if I did look back over it, I'm sure I'd just tear the thing up and throw it away.

But I hope what I'm saying is clear. I know nothing about your domestic circumstances. For all I know, you may have been married or in a permanent relationship for years. If so, I apologize and hope that this letter doesn't cause you or your partner any awkwardness or embarrassment.

But if you do want to meet, call me.
Love, Philip

It was so characteristic of him that Laura almost felt he was in the room with her. The halting style, the continual qualification of everything, the earnestness, the constant feeling of pressure to 'do the right thing', those were the ingredients that made up the only man she had ever loved. And of course it was those same qualities — in particular his at times infuriating decency — that had kept Philip apart from her for nearly twenty-five years.

Laura had no idea whether there would still be any attraction, anything at all left between them. But equally she had no hesitation about her decision. As he had written in the letter, they had to find out. They could not go to their graves not knowing.

She rang him the morning she received his letter. They arranged to meet for lunch in Bristol the following Saturday.

Laura went through a lot of emotions in the intervening five days. As someone who had always prided herself on her control, she was annoyed by how much she vacillated. One moment she thought the idea of seeing Philip was totally ridiculous and could only end in embarrassment; then within seconds her mind had filled with visions of total romantic mushiness. This wasn't what Laura Fisher was meant to be like.

Maybe, she decided, it was hormonal. Her age. Perhaps, although the idea didn't appeal, she should go to the doctor and investigate HRT. That thought prompted another anxiety. Her periods were getting so unpredictable that they could also threaten the weekend's romantic dream scenario.

Laura felt an unfamiliar twitchiness during the

week. Her concentration was bad. Just when she should be channelling all her energies into Lewthwaite Studios, those energies seemed diminished. She did television training sessions with a couple more would-be communicators; she had some preparatory meetings for a corporate video she was directing; but she felt lethargic, on automatic pilot. And she was afraid the clients noticed her ineffectuality.

She really must pull herself together. If Rob ever did emerge from hospital, it would still be a long time before he could be an equal partner in their enterprise. Laura was going to have to run the studios single-handed for a while yet.

The continued presence of Emily in the house didn't improve her mood. Though the girl kept talking about 'my flat up in Clifton', she didn't show much sign of wanting to be there except to sleep. For her leisure hours she had apparently taken root in Laura's house. And her hostess, though she kept trying to make allowances, found the girl's ubiquity extremely irritating.

Laura couldn't understand why it wasn't equally irksome to Tom, but he seemed quite content to sit and listen while Emily made more of her unarguable pronouncements. Maybe it *was* love. Maybe giving up all his independence and initiative to a woman was all her son wanted from life.

Again Laura felt the pang of potential guilt. Was it really her fault? Had her dominant personality sapped Tom's will and left him prey to any other strong-minded woman who fancied annexing his personality?

'We're getting closer,' Emily announced early on the Wednesday evening.

'I beg your pardon?' Laura had just come in from a frustrating day in the studios, where there had been a series of crises which she hadn't controlled with her customary dynamism.

'I said Tom and I are getting closer.'

Closer in a general sense or closer *to* something, Laura wondered, but Emily quickly amplified her meaning. 'I'm going to cook dinner for Tom this evening at my flat up in Clifton,' she announced.

Laura couldn't help herself from saying, 'Oh, what a good little *hausfrau* you are.' She refrained from adding, 'About bloody time too. I'm sick to death of cooking meals for the two of you.'

But she had still said something to offend Emily's politically correct sensibilities. 'No, actually, Laura, it's not the *hausfrau* syndrome. I don't feel any *obligation* to cook a meal for Tom; I *choose* to cook a meal for him.'

'Well, lucky Tom.' Laura looked across at her son, sheepish on the sofa. Since he had met Emily, sheepishness was his habitual expression.

'And Tom's going to stay over,' Emily went on, 'so don't expect him back tonight.'

'Fine,' said Laura, 'though I would have thought you were capable of telling me that yourself, Tom.'

'Well, yes, I . . .' A deep blush now overlaid his sheepish features.

'We didn't want you to worry, so we thought it better to tell you,' said Emily, 'and really, Laura, when two people are —' out came the crook-fingered quotes '— an "item", it doesn't really matter which partner passes on relevant information, does it?'

Philip had used the word 'partner' in his letter, Laura was reminded. To describe some conjectural rival for her affections. She felt a sudden urge to touch Philip, to know if his skin still made hers tauten with desire. She was being stupid, she must stop this dreadful mawkishness.

Then Laura realized what Emily was actually telling her. A statement was being made. Tonight was the night. Tonight Tom, having established his credentials as someone responsible in his attitude to their relationship, was going to be allowed the inestimable prize of safe sex with Emily.

Rather him than me, was Laura's first reaction. After that came a surge of anger, at the idea of this smug little girl moulding and manipulating her son as if he were just a cipher. Emily kept going on about the importance of treating people as people, but in practice her ambition seemed to be the total depersonalization of Tom.

Laura was angry enough to have said something, but another thought stopped her. Was she, after all, in any position to criticize Emily? Though for different reasons, that night in October 1973 she had treated Tom's father as an object rather than as a person.

'Michael hasn't been in touch again?'

'No.'

'Good. I've tipped off a few people to keep an eye out for him. You should be all right.'

'Are you saying that he's really dangerous?'

'Yes,' said Kent, and turned his attention to his steak.

It was the Wednesday evening, one of their regular meetings. Always in the same Steak House. Kent retained his suspicion of 'tarted-up' food. A plain medium-cooked sirloin steak with chips 'and none of that garnish rubbish' was what he favoured. Laura usually had the same. The Steak House's attempts at more exotic dishes were unreliable.

She glanced across at her brother and suddenly realized how old he looked. Only fifty-two, but he could have been ten years more than that. He had thickened out, his neck now the same width as his face. The hair was grey, cut so short that it was hard to tell where he was balding. Looks apart, though, he had hardly changed at all. Still as impassive, still rigidly self-contained, still taciturn, but for Laura his company was still strangely relaxing. Kent was a rock that had always been part of her landscape.

'Viv'll be relieved. Tom's got a girlfriend,' she announced.

'Ah.' The usual even monosyllable, a reaction which gave no clue as to its nature. Kent could have been delighted at the news, furious, or completely indifferent. There was no way of telling. Not for the first time, Laura wondered what it would take to make her brother show an emotion. The last time she had seen Kent lose control, he had been about eleven. He had come in from school and found his father making love to her. No, 'making love' was never the right expression for what that man did. 'Abusing', that was the only word. Even now, over forty years later, Laura felt nauseous at the recollection.

It had been the first time. Not the first time her father had touched her like that, but the first time Kent had seen them together. His own abuse, Laura had gathered later — though Kent never actually talked about it — had already started before that.

The boy's reaction had been terrifying. Shouting, screaming, he had launched himself at their father and, for a moment, in spite of the disparity in their size, it had looked as if the boy might prevail. But, after the initial onslaught, superior strength and violence had ensured the predictable result.

Kent had been beaten unconscious. For once their father's middle-class caution had been forgotten. But of course it had to be kept secret. As ever, Mrs Fisher closed her mind and her suburban net curtains over the incident. Kent was kept away from school for three weeks until his bruises were no longer visible. When he went back, his teachers and class-mates commiserated about his mumps. That was the excuse for absence with which Richard Fisher had made his wife ring the school.

Thereafter, though Kent often fought to keep his father away from Laura, he never again shouted or screamed. He kept his thoughts bottled up; the only means he had of countering his father's attacks was matching, but inadequate, violence.

'I'm afraid I don't like her,' Laura confessed. 'The girlfriend. Emily. Maybe that's just a natural maternal reaction.'

Kent didn't offer an opinion on this. Laura tried to visualize what might be happening at that moment in the bedroom of a flat up in Clifton, but her imagination was unequal to the task. Strangely, the thought of Tom and Emily in bed together didn't disturb her at all. It just seemed rather incongruous.

'Still, I suppose I should be glad,' she continued, accustomed to maintaining a monologue in Kent's presence. 'At least it means the boy's normal, and that's a kind of relief.'

'How do you mean?'

'Well, given the circumstances of our upbringing . . . you know, our . . .' Once again, to her fury, she found she couldn't look at Kent as she said the word '. . . *father*, and so on, it's nice to know that it hasn't carried on into the next generation . . . I mean, if Tom's out there forming relationships . . . well, that's good, isn't it?'

'Good to know someone in your bloody family

can,' said Kent, atypically direct.

'What do you mean?'

'Well, come on, your track record's not that great, is it? Hardly a champion in the relationship stakes, are you?'

Laura was taken aback by this sudden offensive, but Kent had not finished with her yet. 'Oh, you aspire to normality, you behave like there's nothing wrong with you, but deep down you're irretrievably damaged. You're incapable of sharing your life with someone else.'

'Kent, being a couple is not the only possible way of getting through life. Has it occurred to you that my single state might be a positive choice on my part?'

'That's just a sour grapes reaction.'

She was incensed. 'Is it? I see. So everyone has to be half of a couple, do they? That's the rule? Sounds like a form of fascism to me.'

'I'm not saying everyone should. I'm just saying that you'll never be able to.'

'And you say this from the smugness of your marriage, do you — from the safety of the perfect relationship you have with Viv?' She had tried to keep the sneer out of her voice, but failed.

Kent coloured and said quietly, 'Viv and me works. Neither of us has illusions about it. We just tick over.'

'Well, perhaps I wouldn't be content with a relationship that just "ticked over".'

'So you've decided it's better not to have any relationships at all.'

'No, Kent, you're wrong. I do have relation-ships. I have friends. I have Tom. I have Rob.'

'Yes, your only close friend's a bloody wooftah. Everyone else you hold at arm's length. You've never got anywhere near to a real relationship.'

'What do you mean by a "real relationship"?'

'I mean the love thing, the sex thing between a man and a woman. You'll never have that. Our . . .' Even Kent couldn't bring himself to say the word. '*He* ruined the possibility of that for us.'

'For *us?*'

'For you, I mean. It's harder for women to get over that kind of thing. He ruined your chances of ever having a satisfactory relationship.'

'No, he didn't.'

'Well, come on then, Laura,' Kent almost jeered. 'Give me a list of all the satisfactory re-lationships you've had. Where shall we start? Michael?'

'No, not Michael.'

'Who then? All right, you found a man to get you pregnant so's you could have Tom — does that one come under your definition of "a sat-isfactory relationship"?'

'No.'

'Which seems to prove my point.' Once again he spat out the words, 'Irretrievably damaged!'

'You don't know everything about my life, Kent . . .'

'There's not a lot I don't know.'

'You don't know that I have had a good relationship. A loving, fully sexual relationship.'

'You're fantasizing. When could you possibly have had that and me not know about it?'

'When I was in New Zealand.'

Kent looked thunderstruck, then disbelieving. 'What — twenty-five years ago?'

'Yes. I met a man there. It was everything a love affair should be.'

'Then why didn't it last?'

'Because he was married.'

'Oh, how convenient.' His voice grew dismissive. 'Sounds like a comfortable fiction to me, Laura. Stay with it if it helps you get through this shit-hole called life — so long as you don't expect me to believe there's a word of truth in any of it.'

'There is more than a word of truth in it, Kent. The man exists. And in fact he's now in England. I'm going to see him on Saturday.'

All the colour drained from his cheeks as Kent stared at his sister in amazement.

SIXTEEN

She was at Lewthwaite Studios on the Thursday morning when the call came through from the university. Tom's tutor sounded diffident, uncomfortable, but also resentful. He was a serious academic, he didn't feel he should be having to deal with this kind of embarrassment.

'Mrs Fisher . . . ?' he began.

Laura had long since ceased to bother going through the 'Actually it's Miss Fisher' routine and just said, 'Yes'.

'Mrs Fisher, we haven't actually met, but my name is Chris Gregory. I'm Tom's tutor.'

'Oh yes, he's mentioned your name.'

'Good. Erm . . . Well . . .' He dried up.

'I'm sorry, I must ask you to make it quick, Mr Gregory. I am in the middle of a studio session.' She waved reassurance through the glass at the local councillor who vainly hoped her training course in on-camera technique would cure his stutter.

'Yes, Mrs Fisher, right. Well, there's no nice way of telling you this, so I'll just have to be blunt. I'm afraid a complaint has been made against your son.'

'Against Tom? What kind of complaint?'

'A complaint that he attacked a fellow student.'

'Tom? But that's most unlikely. I mean, he's the least aggressive person I know. I suppose maybe if some drunken man picked a fight with him he'd retaliate, but —'

'The complaint did not come from a man.'

'What?'

'It was made by a female student.'

'And what's Tom supposed to have done to her?'

'Beaten her up, Mrs Fisher.'

As the full implications of this body-blow sank in, Laura was silent, and Chris Gregory continued, 'This is the kind of allegation that I'm afraid we have to take very seriously indeed — particularly in the current climate. There's been so much publicity recently about violence against women and date-rape cases and all that sexual harassment stuff, that it can't just be shuffled under the carpet or put down to youthful high spirits as it might once have been.'

He sounded almost wistful for that less egalitarian but simpler time. 'There are enough feminist groups amongst the students — and indeed even more among the staff — to ensure that something like this won't go away quietly. I just hope to God the tabloid press doesn't get hold of it. I also hope that any enquiry and, if necessary, disciplinary action can be kept as a private matter within the university. However, I'm not optimistic. There has already been talk of criminal charges.'

Laura had by now sufficiently recovered from

her shock to ask, 'From whom?'

'From the victim.'

'Who is the victim?' Laura asked wearily. The question was a formality. She knew the answer.

'A girl called Emily Howard. I think you've met her. She and Tom have been going round together for a while.'

'Yes, I know the girl you mean. What happened?'

'Well, I don't have the full details. The procedure within the university is that a student requiring to make a complaint of this kind — or any kind, come to that — should first approach his or her tutor. That's what happened this morning. Emily Howard went to see her tutor — who unfortunately is one of the rampant feminist brigade . . .'

He paused, regretting his lapse into prejudice, and tried lamely to cover it up. '. . . but, nonetheless, a very fair and responsible woman. So, anyway, everything I know comes at second hand from Emily's tutor, who rang me as soon as the girl had spoken to her. The tutor's call was a kind of warning shot — so that I should be prepared for the . . . for the mayhem that's about to be unleashed.'

He was silent, again letting Laura feel his repugnance for the role into which he had been forced.

'So what was Emily's actual allegation against Tom?' she asked.

Chris Gregory cleared his throat, swallowing

embarrassment, and answered, 'Apparently, last night the two of them went to bed together . . .'

'Nothing wrong with that.'

'No, I agree, and no university in the country would dream of trying to stop its students going to bed together. But, *if* you'll allow me to finish, Mrs Fisher, I will explain why this case is rather more serious.

'According to Emily Howard's account, in the course of their love-making, Tom became violent and started hitting her.'

His words brought to life the nightmare which for years Laura had tried not to contemplate. 'But why?' she managed to ask.

'That I don't know yet. One would assume it was the usual kind of scenario. Girl apparently says yes — boy gets excited — girl either never meant yes in the first place or changes her mind and tries to signal no — boy by then out of control and uses violence to get what he wants.'

This was Tom who was being discussed, Laura had to keep reminding herself — Tom, her son, the perfect blond-haired child on whom she had lavished all her love. Tom had committed a crime of violence against a woman. But what crime? 'Are you talking about rape, Mr Gregory?'

'Emily Howard did not actually claim she was raped, no — and I'm sure if she had been she would have done — but the allegation of violence remains a sufficiently serious one.'

'Yes, I can see that. How badly was she injured?'

'I haven't seen the girl, so again my only information comes through her tutor, but apparently Emily suffered extensive bruising round her face and shoulders.'

'Did she need medical attention?'

'No.'

'So it can't have been that bad.' The words came out before she could stop them.

'Mrs Fisher, if you think the relative mildness of the attack in any way exonerates your son from —'

'No, I don't. I don't think that. I didn't mean that. So . . . what happens next?'

'Well, an internal investigation will start here at the university as soon as it can be arranged. It's possible that Tom will have to be suspended during that investigation.'

'Does he know that's a possibility? Does he know about Emily's accusations, come to that?'

'I've no idea, Mrs Fisher. Tom has not come in for his lectures this morning. One of the reasons for my call is so that you can tell him to contact me as a matter of the utmost urgency. Presumably he'll come home to you at some point.'

'Presumably. He might be there now.'

'I've tried your home number, but there was no reply.'

'Right. Well, I'm sure we'll be in touch again soon, Mr Gregory. Thank you very much for letting me know the situation. I'm sorry that you've been dragged into all this.'

'Not half as sorry as I am, Mrs Fisher. My

purpose in being at this university is to pursue serious academic research, and I resent intrusions on my time by students unable to control their animal instincts. Goodbye.'

Laura sat dazed after he had rung off. She returned the telephone receiver slowly to its cradle. Her first instinct had been to think Emily had made the whole thing up, that her allegations were part of some obscure feminist agenda. But Laura couldn't convince herself. This was real. There was no question about it; Tom had attacked the girl.

That knowledge lifted the lid on all the fears Laura had for so long managed to suppress. At times, as Tom grew up, she had felt confident those fears would never return, but this one phone call had revived them instantly in all their horror.

Maybe the evil *was* innate. Maybe the 'bad blood' Kent had spoken of was now bubbling to the surface. The genetic history was too strong. A boy whose father and grandfather had both murdered women would never be able to separate sex from violence.

'B-b-b-bad news?' asked the local councillor from inside the studio.

'No. No, no problem,' said Laura Fisher. 'Let's get on.'

She knew he was there the moment she let herself in through the front door. Laura had left the studios the minute the stutterer's two hours were up, telling Andy there was some work she

182

had to do at home. Her long-cultivated habit of professionalism would never allow her even to hint at any domestic problems. As usual, she had walked briskly up the gradient, cutting across the corner of Brandon Hill Park, to her house.

She moved silently up the stairs. There were small sounds coming from Tom's room, cupboards being opened, clothes rustled. She stood in the doorway. He was instantly aware of her and spun round. On the bed were a beige cardboard folder and an open sports bag, into which a jumble of garments had been hastily shoved.

Tom's expression was haunted, flustered, but at the same time defiant. 'Why aren't you at work?'

'I had a call from Chris Gregory.'

'Oh, right. So you know everything?'

'I don't think I know everything. I only know what he's told me.'

'And that was enough to make you leave work and come to look for me? I'm flattered.'

'What do you mean by that?'

'Just that it's been pretty rare over the years for anything to do with me to be important enough for you to "leave work".'

'Tom, I've always seen to it that you were properly looked after.'

'Oh yes. "Looked after." By someone. Someone who was efficient — ideally someone who was as efficient as you were, though there weren't many of those around. And everyone kept saying, "Isn't it wonderful how Laura manages to hold down that stressful career and look after her son at the same time?" And none of them realized that you didn't do that at all. You held down the stressful career, but you didn't look after your son. You had him looked after.'

Laura was stunned by the sheer bitterness of his onslaught. And though Tom was furious, these weren't rash words said in the heat of anger. They were the product of many years' resentment.

'But, Tom, I never realized —'

'No, you never realized anything. You got your baby, your nice designer baby — the perfect accessory for the successful career woman — and you organized its welfare. Saw that it had enough to eat, nice clothes to wear, schools to educate it, and you never for a moment thought you had to do any more.'

'Tom, that's not true. I've always loved you.'

'Oh yes, you probably have in your way. Yes, I've never lacked for you telling me you loved me, on the rare occasions when we met . . . but I didn't ever see so much of the day-to-day nurturing, did I?'

'You know I've had my work. I've had to pay the bills. And we always had holidays together and —'

'I was never part of your life!' He spat the words out. 'No one has ever been part of your life. I was always just an accessory. A convenience. Something you wanted to have to prove to yourself that you were human. Well, you may have proved it to yourself. I still have grave doubts on the subject.'

'I don't know why you're talking like this.'

'No. I don't think you do. You think you've done everything all right. You're so selfish you can't see anything from anyone else's point of view.'

'I'm not selfish!'

'What? I can't think of anything more selfish than going out to pick up a man to get you pregnant.'

'You don't know that's what I did.'

'Oh yes, I do. And his identity was totally irrelevant to you. Just as mine is.'

'That's not true, Tom.'

'No? All right, tell me. What do you know about me? Except for the fact that I am your son, *the* son, the *item* you so desired. What do you know about my personality? What do you know about what goes on inside my head?'

'Well, I —'

'Nothing. You know absolutely nothing about me. And the reason for that is that you aren't capable of making relationships.'

This was the second time in as many days the same accusation had been made. Laura tried to defend herself. 'That's not fair. I'm not —'

'You hold everyone at arm's length. You don't give any of yourself to anyone.'

'But —'

'And then you're surprised that I'm the same, that I have difficulty in forming relationships with

185

women, that I can't reach out to someone else. These things are hereditary. You can't break the cycle.'

'Yes, you can.'

'No. You can't change the nature you were born with.'

'You can, Tom. That's the whole point. You can.'

'You can't! What happened last night . . . yes, what Emily has gone blubbing to her tutor about . . . that proves you can't change. What happened was inevitable. That's what I'm like. That's the sort of person I am — however much you thought you could break the mould and re-create me in the nice middle-class image of the son you always wanted!'

'Tom, please calm down, and just talk.'

'Nothing more to talk about.' He turned and picked up his bag, pushing in the trailing sleeves. He grabbed a thickly stuffed folder that lay on the bed. 'I'm going.'

Laura barred the doorway. 'You're not going till we've talked through the —'

The power with which he pushed her aside winded her. Being slammed against the door-frame jarred her spine.

'Tom,' she called after him weakly, as he disappeared off down the stairs.

The impact of the front door closing juddered right through the house. Laura sank slowly down the door-frame to sit on the floor. And for the first time since her teens, she let go, and cried.

SEVENTEEN

She lay there for a long time. Sobs shuddered through her body and her eyes streamed as though their reservoir of tears was bottomless. For so long Laura Fisher had held herself together, had convinced herself of the rightness of what she was doing, that the release of that rigid constraint was devastating.

The main blow was to her confidence. She had always thought she was doing right by Tom, that her love for him had communicated itself by the way she had arranged his care. To discover that for nineteen years he had felt himself the victim of emotional neglect hurt Laura like a physical injury. The knowledge struck at the very basis of the life she had created for them, and cast doubt on the validity of every other decision she had made.

Above all, there was the sickening certainty that she did not know her son at all. The child she had nurtured and felt close to, from perfect baby through blond childhood to uneasy maturity, was a stranger to her. All the accumulation of negative thoughts, which she had for so long shut out of her mind, came flooding in unrestrained.

It was maybe an hour after Tom's departure that Laura finally made it to her feet again. Her back ached from its collision with the door, and her whole body felt uncertain and trembly, the body of an old woman.

She rooted in one of Tom's drawers for a handkerchief and wiped it roughly against her smarting eyes. Her son kept his room very neat, put away his own clothes, changed his bed-linen, dusted and hoovered it all himself. That had been part of their deal when he came back to live at home. He had always been an amenable child. When Laura heard what other parents had to put up with from their offspring . . . Tears threatened again. She thought she had brought him up right, but his outburst showed she had failed completely.

Tom felt himself to be alienated, a misfit, unable to cross that seemingly insuperable bridge which separates one human being from another. 'No man is an island . . .' Well, maybe the Fisher family were the exceptions that proved John Donne's rule. Was Tom doomed to live for ever in isolation? And were his words about his mother true? The words that were a paraphrase of what Kent had said the previous evening? Was Laura also incapable of relating to another person?

Suddenly she felt ridiculous about the hopes she had been unable to suppress for her meeting with Philip that weekend. There was no chance at all, no chance that there would be anything left for two people of their age after twenty-five years. Particularly when one of them was an emotional cripple, incurably damaged by the horrors of her childhood.

Laura kept hearing again sentences and phrases from Tom's denunciation. What really struck her was how long he had kept it all in. She had never for a moment suspected that he harboured any such thoughts. But then, as Tom had asked, 'What do you know about what goes on inside my head?' And he had supplied the answer himself. 'Nothing.'

Another of his sentences came back to her, something that had struck a strange, discordant note at the time. 'I can't think of anything more selfish than going out to pick up a man to get you pregnant.'

Maybe it had been a shot in the dark. Tom knew that someone must have fathered him. Equally, he knew of no continuing sexual relationships in his mother's life. Perhaps he had put the two facts together and guessed at a solution. But something about the way Tom had spoken suggested a more detailed certainty.

How could he know, though? No one knew. There were few secrets between Laura and Rob, but she had not even told him. And Kent could have no inkling. Even when she first found out the man's identity from Kent's newspaper in Queen Charlotte's Hospital, Laura had suppressed all reaction to the shock.

She had often wondered how she would have reacted to the straight question from Tom: 'Who is my father?' She had decided she would have replied, 'He was someone whom I met and was very attracted to. We only spent one night together, but I didn't get pregnant by accident. I wanted to get pregnant. You were wanted, Tom.'

She was determined that that was all she would say. She could not bear the idea of Tom knowing that his father had been a murderer. That knowledge would have put far too much strain on a growing boy. The direct question, however, had never come up. Tom had remained apparently incurious about his origins. And yet now it seemed that he did know something.

Laura thought about her son and realized how depressingly right he had been. She did know very little about him. Only the externals. He was nineteen years old. He frequently seemed passive and lethargic, which got on her nerves. And he was doing a degree in media studies, with ambitions to be a journalist. Until Emily came along, except for his occasional unexplained absences, he hadn't seemed to have much of a social life. When he did go out, it was either to lectures and tutorials or with some vague, throw-away remark about 'research'.

Research . . . Was it possible that Tom had actually been researching his own background? That, secretive as ever, rather than asking for information, he had set out to find it himself?

Laura started to search his room. She eventually found what she was looking for in a box-file under the bed. She sat on the duvet, unclipped the file's lid and took out a sheaf of photocopies.

Mostly they were newspaper cuttings, neatly sorted into bundles clasped by bulldog clips. Full marks to Tom's tutors. He was being well trained in journalistic efficiency. The subject of the cuttings, though, sent an appalling chill through Laura. The first group, palely photocopied from fading newsprint, dated back to 1958. They all concerned the trial of Richard Fisher for the murder by strangling of his wife.

Laura had not seen many of the reports before. At the time she had been protected from them by the social workers who were looking after her. Now she read dispassionately of the violent marriage painted by the prosecuting counsel and her father's unconvincing protestations of innocence relayed by the defence. His claim that he had found his wife strangled when he got home from work was given short shrift.

What struck Laura forcibly was how wrong a picture of her mother emerged from the proceedings. Of course Mrs Fisher had been the victim of the crime, but she came across as all victim, nothing more, an innocent crushed by the cruelty of an evil man. No impression came across of her glacial self-control, her obsession with appearances.

Though Laura hadn't been aware of it at the time, she had since rationalized that her mother had probably been frigid. Mrs Fisher had always had a distaste for the messiness of bodily functions, and probably regarded the production of two children as the complete and final discharge

191

of her sexual duties. Though Laura was disinclined to accept any mitigation for what her father had done, she could recognize that his wife's coldness might have been a trigger for his behaviour.

And she could never forgive her mother for the passive acceptance of what was going on. No, it was more than passive acceptance. It had been the positive closing of Mrs Fisher's mind. She literally did not know what she did not want to know. She ignored all evidence of the abuse her children were suffering. So long as her husband kept his hands off her, and so long as she was able to maintain her well-dressed and well-heeled middle-class lifestyle, Mrs Fisher had been content.

She had laid down the ground-rules for their marriage, and Richard Fisher had conformed to them. Contrary to the impression given at the trial, he had never — until the final explosion of anger — turned his violence against his wife. The public image they always projected was of a perfect couple, which was why the murder produced such shock-waves amongst their acquaintances. At social events they were much given to overt displays of affection, and only their children knew that they never touched each other when they were alone.

Laura had often wondered what it was that had broken this arrangement, which parent had stepped over the boundaries of their circumscribed relationship and exposed the violence that lay beneath. But she would never know what had been said that day, what had driven her father finally to put his hands round his wife's neck and choke the life out of her.

There had been no doubt in the jury's mind that that was what he had done. His conviction had been inevitable. So, in 1958, had been his death sentence, though on appeal that had been commuted to life imprisonment. The fact that Richard Fisher had not been hanged had caused considerable outcry at the time from those of less liberal persuasion, and prompted argument in leaders and correspondence columns. All of these too had been neatly photocopied and added to Tom's archive.

Laura put the cuttings down, still trembling with shock. So . . . Tom knew about his grandfather. All her attempts to keep the truth from him had been in vain. Her son was aware of his inheritance of bad blood.

She turned with trepidation to the second bundle of photocopies. First to catch her eye was a photograph of Melanie Harris, the same portrait that had been pinned up in the *Newsviews* office the day after the girl's death. And the day after Tom's conception. The press coverage had been extensive and Tom appeared to have tracked down all of it. Why? Laura wondered savagely. What on earth had drawn him to the case? How could he possibly know it was in any way connected to him?

It was when she saw the *Evening Standard* clipping Kent had shown her in the hospital that she understood. Though legal ethics did not allow the identification of the man as Melanie Harris's murderer, there was an inference that could be drawn through the cuttings which might point to him. She felt certain that Tom had drawn that inference.

And she herself must have been guilty of bringing the case to her son's attention in the first place. Flying in the face of her instincts, Laura had found herself unable to destroy the cutting from Kent's paper. This had not been for reasons of sentiment, but of intrigued fascination. Over the years she had kept meaning to throw the clip away, but never got round to it. Tom must have found it one day. God knew, he had been around the house often enough when his mother wasn't there. He had discovered the photograph and been sufficiently curious to want to know more. It must have challenged his journalistic instincts.

So now Laura could safely reckon that Tom knew the history of bad blood on both sides of his family. She wondered how long he had known, and what kind of pressure that knowledge must have put on him. What had happened between Tom and Emily the night before appeared now in a harsher, more frightening light. Kent had been right. The past was inescapable. Patterns of violence are inevitably destined to repeat themselves.

The worst surprise of the box-file was right at the bottom. On a blank sheet of paper Tom had stuck five photographs. Three were photocopies from newspapers, two were ordinary snapshots. What was striking about the five faces was how alike they all were.

The first picture was a newspaper one of Mrs Fisher, a blurred version of the photo that used to stand on the mantelpiece of Laura's Pimlico flat. The second was of someone Laura had never seen before, though its likeness to the others gave the face an unnerving familiarity. The girl was probably about twenty. The cut of her hair and her make-up — black lines on upper eyelids set in relief by a paler tone above — suggested the picture had been taken in the late sixties. The original cutting had been snipped unevenly along the bottom, so that all that remained of its caption were the words, 'Pauline Spanier, seen at a —'

The third was a snapshot of Laura, one which Rob had taken at a *Newsviews* Christmas party back in the early seventies. The fourth was the newspaper portrait of Melanie Harris. And the fifth was a colour polaroid photo of Emily.

EIGHTEEN

Chris Gregory's voice was even more full of resentment when he rang the studios on the Friday morning. 'Have you seen your son, Mrs Fisher?'

'I saw him yesterday, yes.'

'And I hope you told him how urgent it is that he should make contact with me.'

'I'm afraid I didn't get the chance to do that.'

'What? Oh dear.' Chris Gregory let out a long-suffering sigh. 'So where is he now?'

'I don't know.'

'For heaven's sake, Mrs Fisher!'

'I'm telling you the truth. I don't know.'

'If you're trying to protect him, I have to tell you it won't work. Tom is going to have to take responsibility for his actions sooner or later.'

'I am fully aware of that. And I'd be telling him so right now — if I knew where he was.'

'Are you saying he's run away?'

'He's left my house certainly.'

'Oh . . .' A glimmer of hope came into the tutor's voice, as he saw the possibility of offloading his unwelcome responsibility. 'So he's a Missing Person and we could call in the police to —'

'He is not a Missing Person. I just don't know where he is at the moment. And I'm sure there are a lot of mothers who couldn't always give you the whereabouts of their nineteen-year-old sons.'

'But the police could —'

'It is not a police matter. Tom is not facing any criminal charges.'

'But he may do. The girl Emily Howard certainly mentioned the possibility of bringing charges.'

'And when she does so, I'm sure we can rely on the police to take the appropriate action. Until then, all we can do is to wait till Tom chooses to put in an appearance.'

'Non-attendance at lectures and tutorials could jeopardize his future at the university, Mrs Fisher.'

'I'm sure he's aware of that. And when he's calmed down, I am sure he will come forward to face the music.'

'Hmm.' Chris Gregory sounded dissatisfied. He was under considerable pressure from Senior Common Room feminists and wanted the whole unpleasant business tidied up as quickly as possible. 'So you're telling me, Mrs Fisher, that you're not worried about your son's disappearance?'

'Exactly, Mr Gregory. That is exactly what I am telling you.'

In one way it was true. Laura had plenty of worries about Tom, but his present whereabouts weren't high on the list. She didn't think he was a suicide risk, and the manner of his packing and departure suggested he had some destination in mind. He was lying low and would reappear when he felt ready to do so.

But that was about the only aspect of her son's life that didn't worry her. His denunciation of the way she had brought him up still hurt Laura like a recent wound. Tom's words had struck at the heart of her philosophy of life, and dismantled the dynamo of self-confidence by which she had been driven since her early twenties. The damage might prove irreparable.

But darker than that anxiety were Laura's fears about Tom's personality. Not just because he was a loner or, as he saw himself, a social misfit. More terrifying was the implication of his words, 'You can't change the nature you were born with.' It was Tom's 'bad blood' that had led to his attack on Emily. As he had said, 'These things are hereditary. You can't break the cycle.'

One thing was certain. Laura's current level of anxiety meant she was in no condition for lovey-dovey nostalgia with Philip. She rang him soon after her conversation with Chris Gregory to cancel — or at least postpone — their assignation. There was no reply from his number. She kept trying through the day with the same result. Probably he was off in one of the libraries researching his book.

But there was still no reply in the evening. Laura felt angry and frustrated, though aware that she had no justification for this reaction. She knew nothing about Philip's life in England. He was free to come and go as he pleased. He might be staying with his daughter Tammy and her cricket commentator husband. He might be anywhere.

But she desperately needed to put him off. She sent an overnight telemessage, apologizing for the change of arrangement. But even as she did so she knew it would be of little use if he wasn't at home that night.

On the Saturday morning she had a call from Kent. 'Michael hasn't tried to make contact with you, has he?'

'No. Why should he?'

'Just he may be in Bristol, that's all. We had reports of a disturbance in a Victoria Street pub last night caused by someone who fitted Michael's description. He was gone before the police got there, but . . . thought I'd check.'

'Well, thanks, Kent, but no, I haven't heard anything from him.'

'You all right? You sound a bit tense.'

'Well, I . . .' For a moment, Laura contemplated unburdening herself to her brother. It was tempting, the thought of sharing her anxieties about Tom. But no, that sort of talk was out of bounds in her relationship with Kent. Besides, it would be tantamount to an admission that he was right in their continuing debate about the rival claims of nature and nurture.

So she contented herself with saying, 'I think I'm just tired. End of a heavy week. I'm finding

199

running the studios on my own pretty tough.'

'Oh?'

Her words had sounded too much like an admission of weakness, so she added, 'Though everything is actually going very well. Just have to put in a lot of hours when you're starting a new business.'

'Sure.' He was silent for a moment, then asked, 'But you'll be able to relax over the weekend? Haven't got too much on, have you?'

Laura could feel he was fishing for information, and saw no reason why she shouldn't give it to him. 'I was meant to be meeting up with Philip today — you know, the one I told you about . . .'

'From New Zealand?'

'Right. But I'm going to put it off.'

'Decided it's a bad idea to rake over old embers?'

'No, I'm just too exhausted this weekend.'

'So you will see him sometime?'

'I expect so.'

'Hm. I must go. I've got to be on duty. But, for heaven's sake, if you hear anything from Michael, let me know immediately. Just ring the station and they'll find me. You've got the number, haven't you?'

When she had finished her conversation with Kent, Laura tried Philip's number again. Still no reply. That could mean anything. It could mean he had got her telemessage and gone out to do his weekly shopping or something. It could mean he hadn't been home overnight and was still blithely preparing for his trip to Bristol. Damn it.

She tried his number again through the morning, till long after the last time he could possibly still be there if he was going to catch the pre-arranged train. At last, reluctantly, Laura reconciled herself to the fact that she'd have to go to Temple Meads station on the off-chance that he arrived. She had no hopes for their relationship — indeed, with her current preoccupation it seemed an intrusive irrelevance — but she wouldn't be so cruel as apparently to stand up someone who had once meant so much to her.

He was meant to be on the 10.15 train from Paddington, due in at 11.58. It was on time.

Laura stood in the ticket hall with her back to the Information Centre and watched the passengers off the London train come through from the concourse. She recognized Philip immediately from the way he carried his briefcase. It was a worn leather one, as ever overfilled with books and papers so that it would not close, and he held it gingerly in the crook of his right arm rather as a shepherd might a sick lamb.

Except for that distinctive mannerism, though, he had changed almost beyond recognition. For a start, his shape was different. In the late sixties he had been of slight build, with the kind of wiriness one can never imagine turning to fat. Time had achieved the trick, however. His features had spread, and he was now a rounded, definitely chubby, almost portly, figure.

The hair had gone on top and tufted thickly round his ears, giving him something of a mad professor look. He wore thick-rimmed glasses, through which he peered with a familiar fussy uncertainty. A shapeless overcoat was open over a shapeless sports jacket, and beige corduroy trousers concertinaed down to scuffed brown brogues. If a casting director had presented him for the role of an absent-minded academic, most television producers would have rejected him as too stereotypical.

When she saw him, Laura was caught by a spasm of shyness. Twenty-five years, she felt sure, had wrought at least as many changes in her. Her dark hair, though controlled by skilful hairdressing, was streaked with grey. The firm outline of her chin, she knew, had slackened. The hips were broader, partly as a legacy of Tom's birth, and it was no longer possible to say with pinpoint accuracy where her waist was.

Laura, who, though she had never loved her body, had always known that the world in general considered her attractive, was assailed by sudden self-doubt. The confrontation with Tom had shattered her confidence about everything. What was she doing here? What possible point could there be in two middle-aged people of declining charms meeting after all these years? For a moment she considered doing a bunk. But it was too late. Philip's vague eye had landed on her and he was moving tentatively in her direction.

'Is it Laura . . . ?' he hazarded. Clearly for him the shock of her appearance was as great as his for her.

She had forgotten how strong his accent was. Somehow in the many reruns of her fantasies over the years Laura had ironed out his cramped New Zealand vowels. 'Yes. Yes, it is,' she said.

They faced each other, swaying slightly, uncertain what should happen next. Then Laura darted her face forward and planted a small peck on his cheek. The skin was bristly, a little cold, but otherwise unremarkable. The contact gave no carnal *frisson* to Laura. Nor, from the blankness of his expression, did it to Philip.

'Your journey was OK?' she asked fatuously. There was no point in going into all the attempts she had made to head him off. He was in Bristol. They would have to make the best of it.

'Yes. Yes, fine. I'm quite impressed by these Intercity trains — compared to the ones I travelled on when I was last over here.'

'Oh yes. Yes, they're not bad.'

'You can't imagine how many times I've visualized this moment,' he announced suddenly.

'Me too,' said Laura.

But there was no magic in their words. They still stood awkwardly facing each other. What they had said seemed simply to emphasize the gulf between them, the great void that divided their long-simmered fantasies from commonplace reality. God, this was going to be embarrassing.

'I've booked in a Thai restaurant that I go to quite a lot. If that's all right with you . . . ? You do like Thai food, don't you, Philip?' This question seemed once again to accentuate their alienation, emphasize how little they knew of each other's lives.

'Sounds good to me,' he said with too much heartiness.

They were still facing each other, rooted to the spot. But it wasn't the immobility of chemical magnetism; it was the torpor of social unease. With an effort Laura managed to take a step sideways. 'Well, um, let's go and get a cab then, shall we?'

The lunch was agony. Small talk had never been smaller. Jerky, like a car with a flat battery, the conversation had continually to be jump-started by prompting questions.

They found out all about each other's work. They discussed the differences new technology was bringing to the making of television programmes. Philip summed up the current state of the industry in New Zealand. Laura, in a manner that bored her even as she told it, described the insane Thatcherite lottery by which the ITV franchises had been reallocated and the destructive effects the changes had had on British television. She even found herself particularizing the details of the BBC's budget deficit. It was desperate stuff.

Neither said anything truly personal, though

Philip provided a few weight and growth statistics for his granddaughter Katie. Laura didn't even mention she had a son.

Neither wanted sweets, but they ordered coffee. When it arrived, Laura dared to sneak a look at her watch. God, it was only twenty to two. It felt like the lunch had lasted four hours.

'I don't know if you'd planned which train to go back on, Philip . . .' It was brutal, but something had to be done to end the awkwardness.

'No, I, er . . .'

'They're quarter past the hour. Saturdays the same as weekdays.'

'Oh.' Philip looked at his watch. 'I suppose if I put my skates on, I could make the 2.15.'

'I'll ring for a cab.' Laura knew she was being ungracious as she hurried away from the table, but something had to be done.

She asked the waiter for the bill on her way back from the telephone, and insisted on paying it. 'After all, you've come all this way, Philip. Least I can do is make it my treat.'

'Well, thank you then. And if we meet up in London, I'll return the compliment.'

Laura nodded and smiled agreement, though nothing would induce her ever to go through another lunch like that one.

Back at Temple Meads they both got out of the taxi. 'I've a bit of shopping to do,' Laura lied. 'I'll walk.'

'Fine,' said Philip.

Back in the ticket hall, they looked at each other and grinned meaningless grins. Suddenly Laura had the familiar prickling feeling that she was being watched. She turned her head sharply, but saw no one she recognized.

'Problem?' asked Philip.

'No. Just thought I saw someone I knew.' She looked up at the big clock. Eleven minutes past two. 'Perfect timing. You'll just make it.'

'Yes,' said Philip. He half-turned, as if to step away. For a moment he was still, his body showing the tug of indecision. He faced her again. 'I'm not going.'

'What?'

'Laura, I am not going like this. We haven't *met*. We haven't *talked* to each other.'

'What else have we been doing for the last two hours then?' she asked lightly, trying to divert the seriousness of his words.

'No, we need to *talk* properly.'

'I don't honestly think . . . I mean, I've got to . . . My son'll be back soon and —'

Philip's face was wide with amazement. 'You have a son?'

'Yes.'

'Are you married?'

'No.'

'Living with his father?'

'No.'

'You must tell me about him. You must tell me all about him. You must tell me everything, Laura.'

He tucked her arm in his and led her out of the station. Laura's first instinct was to resist, but she didn't. They walked past the taxi rank, down the cobbled station forecourt and through the traffic into the city. All afternoon they walked round Bristol, along crowded shopping streets, down by the harbour, through parks and squares. They didn't really notice where they walked.

But all afternoon they talked. Or, to be more accurate, Laura talked. For the first time since Tom's conception she talked to someone about her decision to be a single parent. She didn't give any details of how she had met the father or who he was, but she talked about the pregnancy, moving out of London, Tom's upbringing. She said nothing of her fears for his genetic inheritance, she did not mention Emily's accusations against him, but she did repeat the denunciation her son had made of the way she had brought him up.

And all the time Philip listened. He made the occasional comment, gave the occasional prompt, but most of the time he just listened. And as she talked, Laura felt the long-accumulated tension draining out of her. After her long narrative, she was weak with relief and almost stumbled against Philip.

'You all right?'

'Yes, I'm just . . . I don't know. Sorry. I don't usually witter on like this.'

'You witter away to your heart's content,

Laura. I'm happy to listen to anything you have to say.'

She grinned. 'Be your turn next, I promise. Equal opportunities. Equal wittering rights for both sexes.'

She was suddenly aware that it was getting dark. Her watch showed the time to be nearly five. 'Good God,' she murmured.

'You look tired.' Philip indicated a coffee shop the other side of the road. 'Fancy a sit-down and a cup of something?'

'Yes,' said Laura. Philip started across the road. 'No, come back to the house.'

They approached from Charlotte Street. As they turned the corner, Brandon Hill Park lay shadowy and mysterious ahead. The familiar outline of the Cabot Tower was lost in the darkness. Laura unlocked the front door and ushered Philip in. She paused for a moment in the hall, testing the atmosphere. No, Tom wasn't there. They were alone in the house. She drew the living room curtains and turned back to face him. Philip still nursed his stuffed briefcase under his arm. He looked more than ever like a bemused professor.

They said nothing, but moved together by mutual instinct. Philip's briefcase dropped unnoticed to the floor as they embraced. Their lips found each other, and warmth flowed between their bodies.

The doorbell rang. Laura moved.

'Don't go. Don't answer it.'

'I must.' Even through her emotion, she had not forgotten Tom. This might be him, or at least news of him.

She opened the front door. On the step, a small mauvish bruise fading around her left eye, stood Emily.

NINETEEN

'I thought it would be better if we talked face to face, Laura, rather than you hearing this through a third person.'

Emily sat on the edge of the sofa. Her sweatshirt sleeves were as usual pulled down to cover her hands, but she was not unrelaxed. She had simply taken up her customary pontificating posture. Laura sat opposite her, Philip was sprawled resentfully to one side in an armchair.

'Hearing what, Emily?'

The girl looked cautiously across to Philip. 'Perhaps this is something that we ought to talk about "*à deux*" . . . ?' She enclosed the phrase in her infuriating crook-fingered quotation marks.

Laura was amazed to hear herself saying, 'You can speak in front of Philip. There's no problem. Can I get anyone a drink? Emily?'

'Well, only if you've got any herb tea. As you know, I don't drink alcohol.'

'No, of course you don't. Still no herb tea, I'm afraid. Ordinary tea — even got some China — or fruit juice . . . ?'

'I'll leave it, thank you.'

'Philip?'

'I drink alcohol.'

'Good. White wine?'

'Thank you.'

'Won't be a moment, Emily.'

Laura heard no conversation from the sitting room while she was pouring the drinks. But then she couldn't imagine that Philip and Emily would have had a great deal to talk about.

As Laura passed him his glass, Philip's hand touched hers. Electricity zinged through her. God, why the hell had Emily chosen to arrive at that precise moment? Laura sat down again facing her tormentor. 'All right, fire away. But please make what you have to say as quick as possible.'

'Very well.' Emily looked primly down at her knees. 'I'm afraid, Laura, that I am going to have to press criminal charges against Tom.'

Philip raised a quizzical eyebrow, but Laura gestured that he should be silent; she would explain later.

'I see. Well, that's your decision, and you're entitled to it. I'm intrigued, though, that you use the expression "going to *have* to press criminal charges". Where's the compulsion? Why do you have to?'

Emily's pale blue eyes were wide and ingenuous. 'Well, obviously, for the sake of other women.'

'I beg your pardon?'

'An assault was made on me,' the girl explained patiently. 'A sexual assault. I'm afraid that kind of thing has to be made public, or men will think that they can continue to behave in that way with impunity — just as they have for thousands of years.'

'I see. Perhaps you'd fill me in on the precise nature of Tom's assault on you . . . ? I've never been told the details . . . though I must say from where I'm sitting your injuries don't look that serious.'

'It's not the severity of the attack that matters,' said Emily self-righteously. 'It's the *fact* of the attack. Anyway, you can't see the bruising on my shoulders. It's worse there.'

'So what are you saying — that Tom inflicted these injuries on you in the course of raping you?'

'No.' Emily looked across at Philip, once again questioning whether Laura really wanted him to hear all this.

'Don't worry about him. You go on. How did Tom attack you?'

Laura was pleased to see that Emily had the decency to blush as she replied, 'Well, the fact is, Tom and I were in bed together . . . and suddenly he started hitting me.'

'Come on, I want a bit more detail than that. Did you *say* anything that made him lose his temper? Did you say anything that might be seen as an assault on the notoriously frail masculine ego?'

'No, I didn't.' Emily's voice became smaller and more aggrieved. 'I just reached towards him in a spirit of love and he lashed out at me.'

'Hm. Well, I think you may have to be a bit more specific on the details if the case ever does get to a court of law.'

'It will get to a court of law,' Emily insisted complacently. 'The police are becoming much more sympathetic in cases of violence against women.'

'Yes, yes . . .'

'And it's very important that this kind of incident does get maximum coverage.'

'*Pour décourager les autres?*'

'Exactly.'

Laura wondered why Emily made her so angry. What the girl was saying perfectly echoed her own beliefs. With her family background Laura Fisher was an instinctive supporter of anything that might minimize violence against women. But somehow she didn't trust the sentiments she heard coming from Emily's smug little mouth.

For a start, Laura was instinctively defensive of her son. She would have liked to hear Tom's account of what exactly happened in the bedroom of the 'flat up in Clifton'. And she was suspicious of Emily's motives. She felt certain the girl was being got at, used by her tutor in some intrigue of campus sexual politics. Also she feared that Emily would bring too much relish to her role as feminist martyr. The St Joan of the university, immolated on the flames of masculine insensitivity — yes, Emily Howard would love every minute of that.

'OK,' said Laura. 'Thank you. You say you came to tell me face to face that you're going to press criminal charges against Tom. You've done that, so I don't see why I should detain you any longer.'

Emily did, thank goodness, look a little discomfitted by this. 'Very well, I'll be on my way.'

'Fine.'

'I'll be making a statement to the police in the next couple of days, so the criminal proceedings will then get under way and . . . take as long as they take.'

'I should think that'd be about how long they take, yes.'

Emily's lips pursed. Even someone with her immunity to irony could recognize she was being sent up. 'So . . . I'd be grateful if you could pass on the news of what's happening to Tom.'

'If I see him, you can rest assured I will.'

'If you see him? Why, where is he?'

'I have no idea,' Laura replied.

'But he lives here, with you.'

'*Lived*. He's walked out.'

'Oh, but —'

'Now, I'm sorry, Emily, I really must ask you to leave.'

'Very well.' Emily picked herself up from the sofa, practising martyred dignity. Laura ushered the girl out into the hall and handed her her coat. They didn't speak till the door was open and Emily, more waiflike than ever, stood in the filtered light of a streetlamp.

'I don't know why you resent me so much, Laura. I'm only standing up for my rights. All I'm trying to do is conduct my life on my own terms, as a woman — just as you did back in the seventies.'

Laura bit back the rich variety of responses which sprang to her mind and simply said, 'Goodbye, Emily.'

'Goodbye, Laura.' The girl turned away in the direction of the park and was already dwindling into the distance as Laura closed the door.

She went back into the sitting room. Philip was standing, bewildered, in front of his armchair. 'What on earth was all that about?'

Laura felt herself moistening as she moved towards him. Their bodies came together. His erection was proud against her through folds of clothing. Their lips fused in soft delight. Hands moved intuitively downwards. Hers slid from his buttocks to the front, wrestling with his clasp and zip. His were raising her skirt, sidling through underwear to the nub of her, hooking a finger in the silk of her briefs, pulling them down.

He pushed her, she drew him back until she was against the wall. His trousers crumpled down to the floor. Laura pulled the thickness of his penis free and, raising herself on tiptoe against the wall, crammed him into the sweet welcome of her cunt. Both moaned as he thrust upwards. Laura's thighs arched and thrust back at him. It only took a few strokes and he spurted into her. Her body shuddered in answering orgasm.

She saw his face close to hers, smiling. It was transformed. Now it was the face that had for so long inhabited her fantasies. Suddenly everything made sense.

'Bit quick, that one,' Philip said with a lazy grin.

'It was perfect.' Laura grinned back. 'I think we were ready for it.'

'Has been a longish wait, yes. Next time we'll do it slowly.'

'Mm . . .' purred Laura, as she felt his slowly shrinking penis twitch inside and let the ripples of her own afterglow wash over her.

It was as though they had never been apart. Their hunger for each other, their instinctive knowledge of the other's needs, lasted all through the night.

The age of their bodies seemed an irrelevance. The hair on Philip's chest was now white, his belly round and prominent, but the feeling of his skin remained the same. Laura felt a little charge each time she touched him. Her broad hips, stretch marks and pendulous breasts did not worry Philip either. Indeed they seemed to enhance his pleasure, when he took all of a breast into his mouth and fretted its nipple with the tip of his tongue, or reached a hand deep, deep into her cunt, marvelling at its unfamiliar capaciousness.

As before, their love-making was seamless, a continuum of touching and exploring, punctuated by little swells of orgasm for Laura and the occasional gasping, juddering climax from Philip.

Their sex was redemptive and life-affirming. Laura felt justified. The ache for Philip she had experienced over the years had not just been fantasy. The reality vindicated her hopes.

It was mutual. It was wonderful. This, Laura reflected, is what equality between the sexes is about, neither partner dominant, neither adversarial, each pleased to give, each happy to receive.

They fell into a comatose doze about six, as daylight began to pale the colours of the bedroom curtains. They woke at ten and after another delicious little encounter, Laura rose to make some coffee. Standing in the autumn sunlight of her kitchen, she felt eased, massaged, with all her problems resolved and melted away.

She did not switch on the radio, so she did not hear the news that the body of a girl had been discovered in Bristol. It was only when the police arrived about noon that she heard of the murder. Emily Howard had been found strangled in Brandon Hill Park, only yards from Laura's house. Her body had been discovered amongst the shrubs that surrounded a little ornamental grotto. And the police wanted to interview Tom.

TWENTY

Laura gave the police all the information she knew. She told them of Emily's visit the evening before and, as she did so, the awful truth dawned that the girl had probably walked straight from the house to her death. Laura asked whether the detectives knew the time of the murder, but they were evasive and said it hadn't been confirmed yet.

She also gave them all the information she could about Tom. She confessed that he had walked out earlier in the week after a row with her, and supplied the meagre list of friends to whom he might possibly have turned for refuge. Yes, she admitted, she was aware of her son's previous attack on Emily Howard. In fact it was in connection with that incident that the girl had come to see her.

The two detectives were grave and non-committal, but Laura received the firm impression that Tom was their number one — quite possibly their only — suspect.

'It's important that we contact him as soon as possible, Mrs Fisher,' said one of the detectives, 'so that we can eliminate him from our enquiries.' But somehow she didn't think that was what they really wanted to do. '. . . so that we can nail the bugger' might have more accurately reflected the detectives' attitude.

'I should warn you, Mrs Fisher,' said the other one, 'that you would be very foolish to waste police time by trying to protect your son. We'll find him soon enough, and if you are actually withholding information as to his whereabouts —'

'I'm not. I genuinely have no idea where he is.'

'Very well,' said the detective, clearly disbelieving. 'As soon as you do have any information — or as soon as you remember anything that might be relevant to our enquiries, we're relying on you to get in touch with us immediately.'

'I will. Of course I will.'

The main interview had been conducted with Laura on her own, while Philip sat in the kitchen pretending interest in the Sunday papers. Before the detectives left, they spoke briefly to him, confirming Laura's story about Emily's visit. They asked him about Tom and seemed sceptical of his assertion that he had never met the boy. Then they took his address and said they might need to contact him for further questions.

As soon as Laura had seen them out, she came through to the kitchen, tight-lipped and pale. Philip poured coffee for her as she sank on to a straight-backed wooden chair.

'What's it all about, Laura? That is, if you don't mind telling me . . . ?'

'I don't mind.'

'I mean, it must be nonsense. They must be

barking up the wrong tree. You don't think Tom could have had anything to do with the murder, do you?'

'I don't know, Philip,' she replied. 'I just don't know. I would have said, until the last week, that I knew my son, and that if he suffered from any personality defect it was *lack* of aggression. Now . . . I just don't know.'

'Tell me as much as you want to tell me, Laura.'

And she did. Her initial intention had been to edit her revelations, to mention only non-specific fears of inherited criminality, but once she started talking, it all came out.

She told Philip things she had never spoken of to anyone except Kent. She re-created for him the Fisher family home, the neat, net-curtained façade and the evil that lay behind it. She told Philip how her father had abused his two children, and she told him about her mother's murder. She could see that Philip's middle-class sensibilities were appalled, but could not stop herself from telling everything.

'You didn't actually witness your mother's death, did you?'

'No. That was at least one trauma I was spared. I was at school when it happened. My brother Kent suffered, though. He came back from school and found her body in the sitting room. She'd been strangled.'

'I don't know anything about your brother.'

'There are lots of things we don't know about each other, Philip,' said Laura bleakly.

'True. What does Kent do?'

'He's in the police. Detective Inspector, here in Bristol.'

'Well, for God's sake — ring him! Ring him as soon as possible. He'll be able to find out what's going on . . . you know, if they've got any evidence against Tom.'

Kent was not in his office, but Laura left a message for him to ring her as soon as possible.

'I'm not surprised you were traumatized by what happened with your parents,' said Philip, when she was back at the kitchen table, 'and I can see why you take it so seriously. But I really think you've got the whole business out of proportion with regard to Tom. Heredity isn't everything. Upbringing is at least as important — much more important, actually. And, anyway, the malign influence was only on one side of the family. Tom's father was —'

'No,' said Laura. And to her amazement, she found she was telling Philip about Tom's father. She could see the surprise in his eyes turning to distaste as she spelled out the deliberate planning of her pregnancy, but still that did not stop her.

At the end she asked, 'Does what I've told you make you think less of me, Philip?'

He looked uncomfortable. 'I don't know about "less". It certainly makes me think of you rather differently.'

Yes, of course. Philip was at bottom deeply conventional; news like this was bound to challenge his values. 'What else could I have done?' she pleaded. 'You were the only person I'd ever loved, was ever likely to love, and you weren't available. I wanted a child, and I wanted to get a child without any emotional involvement.'

'Yes,' he said slowly, still trying to fit his mind around the new information. 'Why did you want a child so much?'

'To prove I could have one. To prove I could put the past behind me and start afresh. To break the pattern of heredity.'

She realized the irony of her words, given the current situation, and suddenly she was crying.

'It'll be all right. Really, it'll be all right.' Philip stroked her shoulder. Laura felt a new hesitancy in his touch. She should never have told him. Philip would never be able to come to terms with her past. On top of everything else, she had now ruined the only good thing ever to happen in her emotional life. The tears ran more copiously down her cheeks.

When she was again calm enough to be coherent, Philip asked, 'Putting the genetic business on one side, is there anything else that might make you suspicious of Tom?'

'What kind of thing?'

'Incidents of violence in his past, for example?'

'No, none.'

'Excessive interest in violence? Talking about violence? Writing about it?'

Laura shook her head. Then a chilling thought came to her. 'There is something . . . something

that might, I suppose, suggest a kind of obsession . . .'

'What?'

'Come upstairs. I'll show you.'

Philip put down the sheet of photographs with
a grim shake of his head. 'Doesn't look good.
Hope to God the police never see this lot.'

'Why?' Laura asked feebly. For the first time
since her early twenties, she felt drained of will,
a little woman dependent on the superior strength
of a man.

'Because,' said Philip, 'this looks like the dossier
of a violent obsessive. A collection of clippings
about murders.'

'But Tom's studying journalism,' Laura pleaded
hopelessly. 'This was just him researching his own
background.'

Philip shook his head and pointed to the sheet
of photographs. 'Look, two of these women we
know to be victims of death by strangling. Your
mother . . . and now Emily.'

'Actually, it's three,' Laura found herself saying.

'Three?'

She pointed to the picture of Melanie Harris.
'That was the woman who was killed by . . .
Tom's father.'

'Dear God! And to think there's also a picture
of you in the same gallery.'

Laura felt suddenly cold. For the first time
she believed the possibility that Tom was a psy-

chopathic killer. And that she was on his hit list.

'What about this one?' Philip pointed to the photograph of Pauline Spanier.

'Means nothing to me. Don't know anything about her.'

'Well, I think I'd better find out something about her.'

'How?'

'You forget, Laura, I'm deep into newspaper research at the moment. I recognize this typeface. It's *The Times* — well, the way *The Times* used to be.'

'But you can't check through every single copy of *The Times*.'

'I can narrow it down. The photo looks late sixties, doesn't it? And that'd fit in with the type-face. So I'll start there. Name might just possibly be in the index, anyway. I can do it in the London Library. They've got a complete set of *The Times* down in the basement.'

'But what are you hoping to find?'

'Won't know until I see it, will I? But at least,' he said with sudden vehemence, 'I'll feel I'm doing *something* for you.'

'You don't need to.'

'I do.' His voice dropped, thick and intense, as he said, 'I think you may be in terrible danger, Laura.'

Philip was unwilling to leave Laura alone and would only do so after Kent had rung back and arranged to come round. Then he called a taxi and caught an early evening train back to London. He would start work as soon as the London Library opened in the morning, he promised.

They kissed formally, like family members. It seemed incongruous that these two people had shared so much passion the night before. Philip had become brisk and businesslike, and Laura knew this was because he had not yet redefined his feelings. Providing her with practical help was easier at that moment than assessing what — if anything — was left of their relationship.

Kent, when he arrived, was not encouraging. He looked washed out, grey with tiredness.

'Two detectives were round this morning. Looking for Tom.'

'I know!' he almost snapped at her. 'Of course I know. I'm working on the bloody case, aren't I?'

'Oh. So you can tell me what they've got on Tom — what actual evidence?'

'You know I can't discuss that, Laura,' he said testily. 'It's just, given the complaint the girl made against him after the earlier attack, he's obviously the first person they're going to want to talk to.'

'Yes. Look, Kent, if there's anything you can do —'

'What do you mean — "anything I can do"? Are you asking me to pervert the course of justice?'

'No, of course I'm not, but —'

'Listen, Laura, I'm not going to pretend Tom isn't a suspect. I'm very sorry from your point of view, but that's the way it is. I hope to God he had nothing to do with the murder, but if he did the fact that he's what you'd call "family" becomes totally irrelevant.'

'I know.'

'If he's innocent, the best thing he can do is to come forward as soon as possible. The longer he stays in hiding, the stronger the suspicions about him become.'

'I can see that.'

'And you really have no idea where he might be?'

'Absolutely none. For God's sake, Kent, don't you think that I'm at least as anxious to contact him as the police are?' He nodded wearily, accepting this. Laura felt again the prickle of incipient tears. 'I just can't believe Tom'd be involved in anything like this.'

'Can't you?'

That was all he said, but the two words had wide reverberations. Kent was telling Laura that he had no problems with the idea of Tom as a murderer. It would merely confirm his long-held views about the endurance of 'bad blood'.

He didn't stay long, but assured her that her phone would be monitored and the house kept under discreet surveillance for the foreseeable future. Like Philip, Kent seemed in no doubt that Laura was seriously at risk. At risk from her own son.

She spent a miserable night. Though she was

exhausted from the previous night's minimal ration, sleep eluded her. If she did doze for a few moments, she would quickly be jolted back to life, sweating from some terrible dream image. The waking images were no pleasanter. She felt nauseated, as if there were a physical pain inside her body, a real demonic foetus clawing away at the walls of her womb. The truth was even more hideous. Laura Fisher had actually given birth to a monster.

To be training a brand manager from a yoghurt company in the niceties of television presentation seemed so ridiculous in the circumstances as almost to be a sick joke, but that was how Laura spent the next day. Somehow she functioned. Smiles belied her real feelings. Words totally at odds with her thoughts managed to emerge from her mouth. Neither Andy nor the brand manager was aware of Laura's anguish, nor of the incredible slowness with which the minutes passed for her.

She didn't get away till six. A mournful drizzle had kept up throughout the day and the pavements truculently reflected the glow of headlamps and streetlights. Laura trudged up Brandon Hill and as usual cut across the park to her house. It was only when she saw the area cordoned off by plastic tapes that she realized she was passing the scene of Emily's death.

At the same moment, she was aware of a figure moving out of the adjacent trees and the sound of heavy footfalls behind her. She lengthened her stride, but the footsteps continued to keep pace. Even to get closer. Laura flashed a glance backwards and saw the heavy outline of a man hurrying through the shadows. He was only ten metres behind her. She broke into a run.

There was a muffled shout from the man and the pounding of his feet grew louder. Laura's soles slid on the wet path and she went flying to the ground. She sensed his closeness looming above her. A large hand clasped her shoulder.

TWENTY-ONE

'**You should take** more care, young lady.'

She looked up. The man's face was shaded from the light, but his voice sounded benign. He helped her to her feet. His face proved to be as benign as his voice.

'Why were you following me?' Laura gasped.

'To tell you what a stupid thing walking across this park after dark is. Didn't you know a young girl was murdered here over the weekend?'

'Yes, yes, I did know. Sorry, it was stupid. It's a journey I make so often, I just do it instinctively.'

'Well, don't. I'm a police officer. I'm on duty watching the scene of the crime at the moment, but there won't always be someone here. Live near, do you?'

'That house over there.'

'Ah.' Recognition came into the policeman's eyes. 'You're D.I. Fisher's sister.'

'That's right.'

'Don't you worry about a thing. We got men watching your place.'

While this was comforting, it was also something of a shock. Kent had meant what he said about surveillance. It showed how seriously the risk to her safety was assessed. 'And is the phone bugged?'

'Done today, that was.'

'Did you break into the house or . . . ?'

'D.I. Fisher's got keys, hasn't he?'

'Yes. Yes, of course he has.'

'He'll see to it you're looked after, don't you worry. Useful brother to have, he is.'

'Mm.'

'No, you'll be safe, no problem . . .' The policeman wagged an admonitory finger '. . . so long as you don't do daft things like walking across parks after dark.'

'I won't do it again.'

'You better not.'

She couldn't see any evidence of surveillance when she went into the house, but the policeman had said it was there and she believed him. Maybe he himself had been part of it. Anyway, it didn't make her feel any different. Laura could not remember a time when she hadn't had the feeling that someone was watching her.

The panic in the park had left her even more unsettled. She tried without success to eat, and zapped between television programmes which her mind would not take in. At eight o'clock the phone rang.

'It's Philip. I would have rung earlier, but I haven't got your work number and I don't even know what the place is called, so I couldn't get it through Directory Enquiries. Anyway, I've got something.'

'Are you at home?'

'What? Yes, yes, I am. Why?'

'I'll call you back.'

Laura didn't know precisely what Philip had to say, but instinct told her to keep it from the police if at all possible. She unplugged the sitting room phone, took it into her study and pushed the lead into the fax socket. It was a reasonable assumption that that line had not been bugged. The police had been expecting suspicious calls from outside the house; they wouldn't be anticipating deviousness from its owner.

'What the hell was all that about?' asked Philip.

'Security. My phone line's being monitored by the police.'

'So — ?'

'I've plugged into the fax. Think that'll be OK. Come on, you said you'd got something.'

'Yes.' He paused. 'I found the copy of *The Times* that girl's photograph came from.'

'Pauline Spanier?'

'Right.' Philip was again hesitant for a moment. 'And it's bad news,' I'm afraid, Laura . . . I mean, from the point of view of what we were thinking about Tom's obsession.'

'Tell me.'

'Pauline Spanier was also a murder victim. She was strangled.'

'Oh God . . .' Sobs began to pulse through Laura's throat.

'Her body was found in the central private garden area of a square in Mayfair. In 1967. To be precise, on the 27th of June 1967.'

The shock stopped Laura's sobs. That date had great significance for her. It was the day after she had got married.

TWENTY-TWO

'**It's preposterous,**' said Kent. 'You're just clutching at straws. Anything that'll get your precious Tom off the hook.' He sat opposite Laura in her sitting room, his body hunched defensively against her theory. The glass of wine she had poured stood untouched on the table in front of him.

'It's not that.'

'Yes, it is. I know you. You'd do anything for that boy.'

'Maybe, but I wouldn't —'

'And, incidentally . . .' Kent transfixed her with a pointing finger. 'If you do hear from him, you make bloody sure you tell me straight away.'

'I will. I will. But, please, now just listen to what I'm saying. There *is* a logic to it. If you look at them my way, the murders become a sequence, all triggered by the same thing.'

Kent shook his head. 'I can't be long. I've got to go back to the office and —'

'Listen, Kent. Please. Just let me tell you what I've worked out.'

He emitted a grudging sigh. 'Very well.'

'I've never told you about my wedding night.'

'I should bloody hope not. And if you imagine

233

I'm interested, you must think I'm some kind of pervert.'

Laura ploughed on, ignoring him. 'Basically it was a disaster. First Michael virtually attacked me, then when I fought back he became impotent. He couldn't get it up and, in fury, he left the hotel room and apparently spent most of the night walking the streets.'

'So? What's my reaction to that supposed to be? Sympathy?'

'No, Kent. As you'll probably remember — because you were there — the reception was at the Dorchester, and that's where we were booked in for our wedding night. And it was in a square in Mayfair that the body of Pauline Spanier was found the following morning. On the 27th of June 1967. She'd been strangled.'

In spite of himself, her brother was now paying attention. 'What're you suggesting?'

'I'm suggesting that Michael stomped out of the hotel in fury and hatred. Hatred of all women perhaps — certainly hatred of me, the woman who had, in his mind, exposed him, who had made him impotent. As he walked the streets, seething with rage, he saw a girl who looked a little like me. Enough like me for him to attack and vent his hatred for me on her.'

'You're saying that Michael . . . strangled this girl?'

'Yes. Then move on six years and we have the Melanie Harris case . . .'

'What!' Now he seemed angry. 'What the hell

are you on about? We know who committed that murder. It was the bloke who topped himself in the police cell. For God's sake, I was on that case. I know what happened there.'

'You didn't have proof. The man was never charged.'

'No, but I know the evidence we had that enabled us to bring him in for questioning. Anyway, why do you imagine he committed suicide if he was innocent?'

'I don't know,' Laura persisted, 'but just listen to me. At least listen to my alternative scenario.'

Kent shook his head grumpily. 'All right.'

'After I moved out from Michael, I kept having the feeling that he was watching me, spying on me if you like, to see if I was getting up to anything with other men . . . being unfaithful to him is probably the way he'd have regarded it. Well, on the night of the 17th of October 1973, I did go to bed with another man.'

Kent looked confused for a moment. Then he said, 'Oh. Oh, would that have been Tom's father?'

Laura nodded. 'I think Michael must have been spying on me when I met the man. I saw him the following morning and he made some cryptic remark about knowing everything I got up to. I think he realized what was happening when I took the man to a hotel in Paddington, and once again the rage took possession of him.

'Melanie Harris's body was found in a car park quite near the hotel. I think she had the misfortune to meet Michael that night — and the even bigger misfortune to look a little like me.'

'But . . . are you suggesting that Michael somehow knew every time you had sex and that made him strangle anyone who looked like you?'

'Something on those lines, yes. And I think Tom had made that connection, which is the reason why he collected . . .' She dried up.

'Collected what?'

'Oh, nothing.' Though Laura's own thinking had moved on, she must not forget that, so far as the police were concerned, her son remained their prime suspect. She didn't want to draw their attention to his files of ambiguous research. 'Anyway, yes. I think that, in Michael's increasingly unhinged mind, my having a sexual relationship triggered his homicidal tendencies.'

'But . . .' Kent laughed in disparagement. 'If that's the case, why aren't the last twenty years littered with women's strangled bodies? Surely you've had sex more than twice since you left Michael?'

'I had a sexual relationship with Philip, but that was in New Zealand, so Michael didn't know anything about it. Otherwise there has been nothing.'

Kent couldn't resist the dig. 'Huh. You're the one who kept telling me that all that abuse during our upbringing wouldn't stop us from having normal relationships with the opposite sex.'

'Hasn't stopped you, has it?'

'No, no, of course not,' said Kent, '. . . but

it doesn't sound as though your life has been a fairy story of fulfilment, does it?'

She didn't take issue with him on that, but continued expounding her theory. 'As I say, I have not had a sexual relationship with anyone since Tom's conception . . . until last Saturday night.'

'Philip?'

Laura nodded. 'And on Sunday morning the body of Emily Howard, a girl who is said to have resembled me, was found strangled in Brandon Hill Park.'

Kent was impassively thoughtful and silent, as Laura went on, 'And you told me that someone fitting Michael's description had been seen in Bristol last week.'

'I feel besieged, yes,' Laura said on the phone to Philip the following evening, 'but I also feel certain that I'm right. It's my having sex that brings out Michael's murderous instincts.'

'Hm. Kind of thing that might put off potential boyfriends.' Philip regretted the pleasantry as soon as he had said it. Their own relationship had not been discussed since they had last met, and he wasn't yet ready to bring it back into focus. He moved hastily on, 'Is Kent setting up a search for Michael?'

'No. Kent, while admitting that my theory is neat and contains an unlikely degree of coincidence, remains sceptical. He keeps saying nothing can be decided until they've talked to Tom.'

'And there's no sign of Tom?'

'No.'

'You're still not worried about his safety, though?'

'Not really. I'm still worried about his situation, and occasionally I get these panics that my theory about Michael is rubbish and Tom really did strangle Emily and . . .' She sighed. 'But no, I'm not concerned about his physical well-being. I think he's just deliberately lying low somewhere.'

'Hm. And Kent's still keeping up your protection . . . the surveillance?'

'Yes. And he's round here quite a lot himself. He's behaving as though he thinks something else is going to happen.'

'What kind of thing?'

'Difficult to know. Kent never was the world's greatest communicator. But I assume he must be worried about the possibility of an attack on me.'

'From whom?'

'I'd say Michael. He'd probably still say Tom.'

'Have you got any protection yourself?'

'I've got a gun.'

'Really?' Once again Philip's conventional values were challenged.

'I did a feature on *Newsviews* about how easy it was to procure guns in central London. Ages ago, this is, early seventies. Anyway, it seemed a good opportunity to procure myself one. I've never fired it. Don't even know if it does fire.'

'Hm. Well, you look after yourself.'

'Course I will. I was thinking, Philip . . .'

'Yes?'

'The only way we can advance now — assuming Tom doesn't suddenly put in an appearance — is by finding out more about Michael . . . talking to him perhaps . . .'

'But where is he?'

'No idea. I was thinking, though . . . so far as I know, his mother's still alive.'

'Oh?'

'She was always very devoted to him. That's the basis of most of his problems. I can't imagine she hasn't got some means of contacting him.'

'So, are you going to ring her to find out?'

'She'd put the phone down on me. Never been her favourite person — and certainly wouldn't be now after the way I've treated her precious baby.'

'Laura, do I detect I'm being asked to do something?'

'It would really help. Just see if you can find out where he is, what he's been doing. I'm sorry to ask you, Philip, but —'

'Don't worry. Of course I'll do it.'

Once again Philip was keener to serve Laura by positive action than to explore their emotional relationship.

It was only half past eight when Laura put the phone down, but she felt infinitely ready for bed. No one could continue to live life at the level of tension she had suffered for the previous few days, and her body suddenly gave itself up to exhaustion.

The effort of getting upstairs seemed insuperable, but somehow she managed it. She flopped down on the bed — 'just for a second' she told herself — and her eyes closed. She got more than a second of oblivion, but not much more, as the phone shrilled her awake.

'Hello?' The word was instinctive; her brain had not yet come back to life.

'Hello, "Mummy".' His sardonic tone was unmistakable.

'Tom. Tom, you must come back. Listen, this call's being recorded so they can find out where you're —'

The line went dead.

TWENTY-THREE

'**Why the hell** did you tell him the line was bugged?' Kent's voice on the other end of the phone was furious.

'I thought it'd make him realize he couldn't escape for ever. I thought . . . I'm sorry, I was half-asleep. But you can trace where the call was made from, can't you?'

'Probably,' he grunted. 'Almost definitely be a public call-box, and when we get there, he'll be long gone.'

'Look, if Tom rings again, I won't —'

'Not fucking likely to ring again, is he? Listen, we've been trying to sort things out for you, Laura, and if you don't cooperate yourself, we can hardly —'

'I wasn't deliberately not cooperating.'

'No?'

'What do you mean?'

'Telling Tom the line was bugged could sound, to someone who was a bit suspicious of your motives, like you were warning him off.'

'I wasn't. I just wasn't thinking.'

There was no disguising the anger in her brother's voice. 'If you hear anything from him again, Laura, you fucking well tell me — all right?'

'Yes. Yes, Kent,' she replied, feeling like a naughty schoolgirl, as he slammed the phone down.

Twenty minutes before, she had been prepared to sleep round the clock, but now Laura was totally awake. It would be another long unwinding. She poured a large glass of wine and tried, without success, to focus her mind on some television programme. It was about half an hour later that she heard the fax machine signalling an incoming message. She moved through into the study and read as the typewritten lines advanced out of the slot.

'Dear Mummy,

In sending a fax, I'm taking the risk that there aren't any police actually with you in the house, and that you'll see this first and destroy it as soon as you've read it. If the police do see this message, that'll only mean the end will come quicker.

I know I should give myself up and I know the whole thing will soon be over, but if it's possible I'd like to speak to you alone, just to put my side of the story, to explain to you what really happened. Meet me at the Leigh Woods end of the Suspension Bridge. I'll go there straight from here and wait till eleven o'clock. If you haven't arrived by then, I'll do what I know I should do and —'

Something went wrong with the transmission. The ensuing print broke up into wavy lines, then vanished. The machine's guillotine neatly sliced off the one sheet. Laura waited, but no second sheet followed. Nor was there an attempt to re-transmit the original one. She inspected the paper in her hand. Though the time was printed at the top, there was no originating fax number.

A new cold fear took possession of Laura. She hadn't previously thought there was any danger of Tom killing himself, but the threat was implicit in his message. His choice of rendezvous made the possibility chillingly more plausible. The Clifton Suspension Bridge, with its sixty-metre drop into the Avon Gorge, had always been a magnet for the suicidal.

Kent had ordered her to let him know the minute she heard anything from Tom, but she couldn't tell him this. The arrival of her brother with a posse of policemen might easily panic the boy into jumping. Whereas, if she could talk to him on her own, Laura might be able to calm him, persuade him to give himself up.

She felt the sick terror that had gripped her when Tom had had measles as a two-year-old. He had been very seriously ill and she had known, from the grim anxiety in the doctor's eye and the speed with which the child had been rushed into hospital, that his life was in danger. She remembered the visceral anguish of that time, the prayers to a God she hadn't thought she believed in. Please save him. Even if he's disabled by the illness, please keep Tom alive. The same feelings were echoed now. Even if he has to spend the rest of his life in prison, please keep Tom alive.

TWENTY-FOUR

It was a keen, cold night. Laura drove with obsessive concentration. As she neared the toll booth, she reached into her pocket for the ten and five pence coins she had in readiness. She slowed and wound down her window to slip them in the slot. She heard the spectral sighing of the wind through the metal uprights ahead. The red and white barrier lifted.

The car felt the tug of the wind as it crossed the span of Brunel's magnificent structure. The whole roadway seemed to sway from its suspending chains. The bridge itself was brightly illuminated and, though she could only see spots of lights from buildings around the gorge, Laura could sense the emptiness of the giant void beneath. She looked keenly along the pedestrian walkways and tried to separate the shadows that hugged the windmill-shaped structure of the far pier. But as she went through the arch and past the barriers, there was no sign of any human figure.

Laura parked her car in the lay-by on the right beyond the toll booth. She got out, feeling a new nausea. Surely it wasn't eleven yet. She looked again at her watch. No, just after ten. But still she couldn't lose the sick feeling that she had arrived too late.

As she walked through the low blue metal gate on to the bridge, a car crossing from the Clifton side illuminated her briefly in its headlights. Laura saw the Samaritans' notice on the pier and a new tremor ran through her. She walked on, keeping to the pavement on the toll booth side. The bridge's bright illumination bleached everything to an unearthly pallor. As Laura emerged on to the exposed part of the bridge, the wind scoured her face and plucked at her coat. She was on the rectangular ramparted area that surrounded the tall pier. Another car crossed from Clifton. Still Laura seemed to be the only pedestrian on the bridge.

She moved a little further along the walkway. Now she could feel the wave-like ripple of the huge structure swaying in the wind. The sighing in the suspension rods had grown into a moaning. Through the decorative metalwork of the side wall, she caught the dull glint of reflected light in the water below. Far, far below.

Laura turned round, but still could see no one. Then she walked back and crossed the roadway by the barriers. On the other side was a matching ramparted platform around the foot of the pier. From the wall of that was a sheer drop down to rocks below. Over the wall Laura could see the lights of South Bristol. Her footsteps sounded unnaturally loud against the keening of the wind as she moved cautiously round the pier.

Just as she turned the corner, she was caught

in the glare of another passing car. A human outline stepped out between her and the head-lights.

'Laura,' said Michael.

TWENTY-FIVE

He looked shabbier than ever. The lights shone on his bald head and caught a glint of madness in his eye. Laura backed away as he moved towards her.

'Well, this is a surprise, isn't it?' said Michael, his voice more incongruously patrician than ever.

Laura felt the stone wall suddenly against her back. Still Michael advanced.

'Why have you brought me out here? What do you want?'

'You know what I want, Laura. It's what I've wanted for many years — what I've *needed* for many years.'

He was now close enough for her to smell the sourness of his breath, an amalgam of alcohol and tooth decay.

'And now you're going to give me what I want, aren't you?' He reached out a hand towards her. Laura felt heavy, incapable of movement, as the hand edged closer.

'Get away from her!'

There was a shout and a thunder of footsteps. Michael turned in fuddled surprise to see the tank-like bulk of Kent hurtling towards them. The detective's shoulder slammed into Michael's side and sent him sprawling to the ground. Laura felt the blessed relief of her brother's strong hand on her shoulder. 'It's all right,' he said. 'I won't let him hurt you.'

Across the platform, Michael was easing himself up against the pier. 'Watch out!' shouted Kent. 'He may be armed! Get down!' Laura felt herself hurled across the ground. Her knees were grazed against the stonework, and she lay on her front, winded.

'Keep away from her, you bastard!' she heard Kent shout. Then there was the sound of a blow thudding into flesh, a grunt, a scraping sound, a scream.

When she managed to pick herself up and turn round, Laura saw only Kent, outlined against the parapet. 'Michael . . . ?' she asked feebly.

'He jumped.' Kent was panting heavily as he came forward to help her up. 'I'm sorry I had to throw you down, Laura. He'd got a gun. Thank God he didn't use it.'

When she was on her feet, instinctively Laura put her arms around her brother's neck. Equally instinctively, Kent removed them. Even at a moment of such emotion, he could not cope with physical affection from her.

'At least you don't have to worry any more. Michael's dead. The threat to you has gone, Laura.'

'Yes.' She found herself surprised by tears, tears of relief that the long nightmare was over.

'You OK to drive back?'

Laura shook her head. 'Don't think so. I'm very shaken.'

'I'll drive you. You can pick up your car in the morning.'

Kent had also parked on the Leigh Woods side, a bit further up the hill from Laura's car. As soon as he got in, he was on the car-phone to his colleagues. 'Another body off the bridge. Get men out here quickly. I've just got to drive someone home — she's in a state of shock.' There was a question from the other end of the line. 'Well, let's just say I don't think we're going to have to look any further on the Emily Howard case.'

Kent parked outside the house in Charlotte Street South. Laura was still dazed and in shock, so he used his key to let her in. He poured her a large brandy. 'You going to be all right?'

'Yes,' she said. 'Yes. How did you know Michael was going to be there?'

'I'd been following him. Saw him by chance in the street this evening. I'd got enough to pull him in for questioning, but I thought I'd see what he did next. What he actually did do next surprised me. He broke into an office in Clifton. I waited outside for a while, then went in after him. Found him in the process of sending a fax.'

'The one I got?'

'Yes. The one he pretended came from Tom. He ripped it out of the machine when he saw me, then managed to push past and get away.

250

But he'd left the fax, so I knew where he was going. I rang to try and stop you going to the bridge, but you'd already left.'

'I had to go.'

'Yes. He was clever. He knew if you thought there was any threat to Tom, you'd be there.' Kent looked at his watch. 'I must get back to the bridge. You sure you're going to be all right?'

'Yes. Fine. I'm just shaken. I'll be fine. I'll have a bath and . . . Oh, I'm just so relieved.' Tears once again prickled at Laura's eyes. 'Because this means that Tom's off the hook, doesn't it?'

'Certainly does,' said Kent with one of his rare smiles. He rose from his chair. 'I'll call you in the morning. If you need anything else from me tonight, I don't know how long I'll be out, but you've got the mobile unit number, haven't you?' Laura nodded. 'OK. You look after yourself. I'll take the surveillance off your house. You've got nothing to worry about now, Laura.'

'No.' She smiled, longing to put her arms round her brother and hug him, but knowing that she would never be able to do that. 'Thank you, Kent.'

She was in the bath, the water rather pleasurably stinging the grazes on her knees. A languor was beginning to take possession of her body when she heard the telephone ring. Laura wrapped a towel around herself, went through

251

into the bedroom and lifted the receiver.

'It's Philip.'

'Oh. Hi.' She had no reaction to his voice. She was still too numb from the events of the evening to think about their relationship.

'I've got some information on Michael.'

'Sorry?' She couldn't think what he was talking about.

'Remember, you asked me if I could find out anything about him. I contacted his mother and —'

'I remember, yes. Well, thanks very much, Philip, but it really doesn't matter now.'

'Oh.' He sounded disappointed, deprived of his dramatic moment. 'What do you mean?'

'Well . . .' Suddenly the effort of spelling out the details of the evening's events, coping with the appalled reaction, the expressions of solicitude, seemed insuperable. 'It just doesn't matter.'

'What, even if it's something to do with Emily Howard's death . . . ?'

'Emily Howard's death has now been explained. Michael killed her.'

'No, he didn't,' said Philip.

'What makes you think that?'

'Because I've traced Michael Rowntree's movements over the last week. Last Friday he was arrested for being drunk and disorderly in a pub in Ladbroke Grove.'

'So?'

'So . . . he spent Friday and Saturday nights in a police cell in London. There was no way he could have been in Bristol strangling Emily Howard.'

Laura had only just put the phone down after the call from Philip when it rang again. She picked up the receiver. 'Hello?'

'I'm coming to see you shortly,' said the voice at the other end. 'I've got a big surprise for you.' The line went dead.

Laura shuddered uncontrollably. The caller had been Tom.

TWENTY-SIX

She immediately called Kent on the mobile unit
number. He wasn't there, they said they thought
he had gone home. She left a message to say if
he did come back, could they ask him to come
and see her as soon as possible. She didn't attempt
to make it sound like a brave message; it was
a naked plea.

Maybe he was at home. She rang his number
half a dozen times. The line was continuously
busy. But she was too scared to be alone in the
house. She had to get away. Drying herself unevenly and throwing on some clothes, Laura stumbled out to her car. Once she was driving she
felt a little calmer, though she was still sweaty
and gasping for breath.

Kent was the only one who could help her.
She had to see Kent. Instinctively, she drove down
towards Hotwells. She parked on the steep gradient outside her brother's house. There was no
light downstairs, but a little spilled through a
crack in the curtains of the first-floor master bedroom. Loud music seemed to be coming from
there as well. Laura recognized k.d. lang's 'Constant Craving'.

She pressed the doorbell, but there was no response. She tried again. Still nothing. The music

was probably too loud for the bell to be heard. In desperation Laura reached for her keys and found the one Viv had given her so that she could get in to water the plants. She turned it in the lock.

The hall and the whole downstairs were in darkness. As she entered the house, Laura was aware of an insistent electronic tone coming from the hall table. It took her a moment or two, while her eyes accommodated to the gloom, to identify that the sound emanated from the telephone, which had been left off the hook. That explained the continuous engaged signal.

There was no one on the ground floor, but the music above continued. Laura could have called out, but some instinct told her not to. She moved silently up the stairs. The landing light was not on, but the door to the master bedroom was slightly ajar. Laura glided cautiously towards the line of soft light between door and frame. She brought her face close to the slit and looked into the bedroom. The shock of what she saw made her catch her breath, and she only just restrained herself from exclaiming out loud.

TWENTY-SEVEN

When she got back to Charlotte Street South, Laura went straight to the study. From the recesses of her desk she produced the gun. It was the one she had procured when doing the *Newsviews* feature on illegal firearms all those years before, the one she had pressed against the forehead of Tom's father in the Paddington hotel.

She sat in the sitting room with the gun on the arm of her chair, and waited. The thoughts that went through her head were not pretty. All the old panics about 'bad blood' recurred. Laura felt powerless, caught up in a cycle of violence which could only end in more violence.

She should not have aspired so high. Kent had been right all along. People with their background were scarred for ever. Sooner or later the bad blood would bubble again to the surface. His course — not to have children — had been the responsible one. Perpetuating the malignancy into another generation was an act of wickedness.

She heard a key in the front door, and the sound of its opening. Laura's hand closed over the butt of the gun as she looked towards the doorway from the hall.

TWENTY-EIGHT

'**This is illegal,**' said Kent, weighing the gun in his hand.

'Come on, I've had it for over twenty years.'

'Doesn't make it any less illegal. You should hand it in.'

'Rather hang on to it for the moment.' Laura took the gun from him. 'I feel more secure when I've got it.'

'Why're you so frightened? Surely, now you know that Michael killed Emily —'

'I don't know that. In fact, I know that he didn't kill her.'

'What?'

Laura gave him the information she'd had from Philip.

At the end, Kent looked thoughtful. 'I see what you mean. Yes, it doesn't look too good for Tom, does it?'

'Kent . . .' Laura began slowly, 'what evidence did you ever have against Michael?'

'What?' He waved the question aside. 'It's very technical. Forensic traces and . . . A layman wouldn't understand.'

'No? But you reckoned you had enough to get him in for questioning about Emily's murder . . . whereas in fact he wasn't even in Bristol when the crime was committed?'

'We aren't infallible. The police do make mistakes.'

Laura nodded. 'And no doubt you could find just as much evidence against Tom . . . if you had to . . . ?'

'Well, I . . . What are you talking about, Laura?'

'I was just wondering . . . if Michael had nothing to do with Emily's death . . . then why did he get me to go to the Suspension Bridge?'

Kent shrugged. 'He probably just wanted to borrow some money.'

'If that was the case, why the secret rendezvous? Why didn't he come round here? That's what he did last time he wanted money.'

'Yes, well, who knows what went on in his mind?'

'But why would he set up all that elaborate business with the fax, apparently meant to come from Tom? Did he even know that Tom was missing?'

'People in Michael's state aren't very logical.'

'No,' Laura agreed thoughtfully. Then she said, 'Last Saturday you rang me to say someone answering Michael's description had been making a disturbance in a Victoria Street pub the night before.'

'Mm?'

'Whereas in fact Michael was in a pub in Ladbroke Grove on Friday evening.'

'So . . . ? The information was wrong.'

Laura looked into Kent's eyes. 'I've just been down to your house,' she said.

'What?'

'Down to Hotwells.'

'Why?'

'I was scared. I needed to see you. But you weren't there.'

'No . . .' He looked bewildered. He didn't know where all this was leading.

But Laura knew. 'I couldn't make anyone hear when I rang the bell, so I let myself in. I went upstairs. There was music coming from the master bedroom.'

Kent was now staring at her, an expression of anticipated horror on his face.

'Viv and Denise were on the bed,' said Laura quietly. 'They were making love.'

Kent averted his head as she went on, 'They're not mother and daughter, are they? They never were mother and daughter. Yours has always been . . . what's the expression that's used in these circumstances . . . a marriage of convenience . . . ?'

Kent looked up at her defiantly. 'So why the hell not? We'd known each other in London. Viv and Denise had been together for years. We were moving to a new place with no history. We both knew how nosy and unforgiving people can be if you don't fit into one of their stereotypes — particularly in a gossipy, backbiting organization like the police force. The world is full of couples, you see, and if you become part of a couple, ninety per cent of the world's curiosity about you instantly vanishes.'

'So you and Viv made a deal?'

'To our mutual benefit, yes. We'd get married, we'd pass off Denise as a product of Viv's disastrous first marriage . . .'

'Which never existed?'

'Too right.' Kent let out a bark of bitter laughter. 'She'd never let a man near her.'

'So she and Denise always slept in the master bedroom and you in the spare room?'

'Yes. And we very rarely saw each other. Shift patterns in our kind of work can easily be manipulated to keep two people apart.'

'But didn't anyone suspect?'

Kent shook his head. 'No. As I say, when you're part of a couple, people lose interest in you. Anyway, you and I, of all people, know what can be hidden behind the net curtains of a nice middle-class house, don't we, Laura?'

She looked thoughtful. 'I can see what was in the arrangement for Viv and Denise, but what did you get out of it, Kent?'

'The same as they did. Freedom from prying eyes. Nobody trying to find my dark secrets.'

'What dark secrets?'

He laughed harshly. '*You* have to ask me that. Would it make it clearer if I said *our* dark secrets.'

Laura looked at her brother, and suddenly she understood. 'Oh, my God, Kent . . .'

'What?'

'You sent the fax, didn't you? You lured Michael to the bridge . . . How did you do it? Tell him I wanted to see him? Tell him I'd changed my mind and I was going to give him some money? Oh, Kent . . .'

Her brother was silent.

'I got it right, didn't I?' Laura continued in an even voice. 'About the murderer's motivation. The knowledge that I was having sex put such mental pressure on him that he became homicidal. That was why the stranglings happened. Only thing I got wrong was the casting. I thought it was Michael who was affected like that. But no, it was you, wasn't it, Kent? All the time it was you.'

He sank down into a chair, with his head in his hands. Something between a choke and a sob racked his body.

'Oh, Kent . . .' said Laura. 'Why couldn't you have talked about it?'

'You don't talk about things like that,' he replied in a strangled voice. 'You pretend everything's all right. You go through the motions, you do everything you should . . . until the pressure becomes intolerable, and then you do the only thing you can do.'

Laura looked down pityingly at the knotted muscles of her brother's back under the inevitable grey jacket.

'We were damaged, Laura. We were so damaged. It wasn't what he did to me, I could stand that. It was what I saw him doing to you. It was so cruel. I needed to protect you. And yet at the same time I could feel a bit of what he felt. I could feel the anger, the hatred of women that was in him when he fucked you — the hatred that is perhaps in all men when they fuck women.'

'No,' said Laura. 'No.'

'And with this need to protect you, all the time I also felt the need to hurt you. You were a woman and I hated your sex. I hated the two-facedness of women — the charming, the demure, polite, untouchable bit — and then the hungry, lustful, the greedy . . .' he swallowed '. . . sexuality. And the hatred and the lust and the violence all . . . got mixed up,' he concluded lamely.

'And you felt all this violence towards me?'

'Yes. Yes. Not when you were yourself, when you were innocent and feminine and gentle, but . . . when I thought of you as a sexual being . . . when he fucked you . . . when anyone fucked you.'

'And then you felt an urge so strong that you had to go out and find someone else to . . . take it out on?'

He nodded, almost metronomically. 'And when I'd done it, when I'd strangled the other woman — the woman who was Laura but at the same time wasn't Laura — then I felt better. The pressure was relieved, the thoughts had gone away, I could get on with my life.'

'But you must have known the risks you

were taking. Weren't you afraid of being found out?'

'No.' He smiled with something like pride. 'I was clever enough to get away with it — and of course uniquely placed to get away with it. As a detective I was on the spot, I could control the way an investigation went.

'I can control the way this new investigation at the bridge goes. I can edit my version of what happened to Michael. There won't be any problem. The police like open-and-shut cases.'

'And what about the investigation into Emily's murder?'

'Control that one too. See which enquiries are made, which aren't made.'

'But how could you have killed her, Kent? She was only a child.'

'I had to, Laura,' he replied seriously. 'Had to. I'd seen you going back to Temple Meads with Philip. I thought he was on his way back to London. But when I saw you coming out again, arm in arm, I knew . . . I knew how it'd end up.' He swallowed uncomfortably.

'I saw you when you came back here. I sat on a bench in Brandon Hill Park and . . . the pressure started to build up again. When I saw Emily arrive, I knew what I'd have to do. And when she came out . . .'

The sentence didn't need finishing, but his perverse boastfulness continued. 'And take that man — Tom's father. Once I'd tracked him down it was easy to fabricate enough evidence to have him pulled in for questioning. Easy enough to arrange time alone with him in his cell — and to make it look like suicide.'

'But why did you do that, Kent? Why did you have to kill him?'

'To punish you, Laura.' He looked at her smugly. 'I was very annoyed by what you'd done. You had to be made to suffer for it.'

'So all I went through — all the agonies of thinking my son's father was a murderer — you set that up?'

'Yes,' said Kent. 'Looking after someone is not just being nice to them, you know. Sometimes, if they get out of line, they have to be disciplined. You had to be disciplined. I was being cruel to be kind.'

'So you've been watching me? All the time you've been spying on me, Kent?'

He smiled and nodded. 'It shows how much I care for you. I set up the marriage with Viv so that no one would think it odd my staying down here near you. I've even turned down promotion because it would have meant moving away from you, Laura.'

'But why? Why have you done all this?'

'Because I love you, Laura. I've always loved you.'

'You have a pretty damned peculiar way of showing it.'

'Yes.' He chuckled. 'Yes, I do, don't I?'

'But all those murders . . . The three girls,

Tom's father, Michael . . . Do you realize that's five people you've killed, Kent? Five human lives you've taken away?'

He was confident now, almost preening as he corrected her. 'Six.'

'Six?'

'Our father was capable of abusing us, but he hadn't got the balls to commit murder.'

'You mean, you . . . ?'

Kent nodded complacently. 'I'd seen him fucking you the day before. All the thoughts built up. It was intolerable. I could feel the violence welling up in me. At first I turned it inward, I decided to top myself. I even went downstairs to the kitchen to find the carving knife. And then she came in. She asked what I was doing with the knife and I told her. I told her I was going to kill myself . . . and do you know what she said . . . ?'

Wordlessly, Laura shook her head. Kent chuckled as he spoke, 'She said, "No, you mustn't do that. What will people think? What kind of upbringing will they think we've given you?" And that was so typical of her — pretending nothing was wrong, ignoring the hell he was putting us through. My anger just welled up, and my hands were round her throat before I had time to think about it. She looked very like you,' he reminisced fondly.

'And when I'd done it, when I'd killed her, I felt liberated. It was all right. I now knew what I had to do when the pressure got too bad.' He sniggered. 'And also of course I'd got rid of him at the same time. It was easy for me to invent a history of domestic violence, and the police were more than ready to swallow it. Anyway, I arranged her body so that it looked as if he'd done it.'

'So all the time that our father was protesting his innocence, he was actually telling the truth?'

'I'd never call him innocent, Laura. Not after what he did to us.'

'No, not innocent, but innocent of murder.'

'Well, he got punished for it, anyway. And that meant he couldn't get at you any more, so everything was all right . . . until you married Michael.'

'And then it all started again?'

Kent nodded. The confession seemed to have relaxed him.

'You'll have to tell someone,' said Laura. 'There are people who can help you.'

'Crap! I don't need help. I'm fine as I am.'

'Don't be ridiculous. You know how damaged you are.'

'Oh yes, but I've learned to live with the damage. My whole life, you could say, has been an exercise in damage limitation. And now comes the moment that it has all been leading up to.'

He was on his feet so quickly Laura did not have time to move away as his muscular arms pulled her up towards him. She felt the fierce rigidity of his erection against her.

'I love you, Laura,' said Kent. 'I've always loved you. At last, this is the real thing.'

She tried to move away, but his hands clamped her head to push her lips to his. The hands slipped down to rest either side of her neck. Gently at first. Lightly. Then the fingers stiffened and the hands closed inexorably together.

TWENTY-NINE

It was relaxing, somehow right. And strangely erotic, thought Laura, as the air was squeezed from her and consciousness waned. She was almost disappointed by the commotion, the shouts. She was aware of one of Kent's hands releasing its grip, and then the other. She slipped down to the floor.

She can only have been out a few seconds. When she opened her eyes, she saw Kent standing at bay, holding the gun. Opposite him stood Tom and a bulky youth she had never seen before.

'Either of you make one move and I'll shoot!'

'Don't do that, Kent.' Laura's voice was drowsy and languorous. 'That won't solve anything.' Somehow she managed to pull herself up to her feet. She advanced towards her brother with hand outstretched. 'Give me the gun, Kent.'

'I'll shoot you.'

'No,' she purred. 'That's not your method. That wouldn't be half as much fun. Come on, hand it over.'

Kent stood for a moment undecided. Then, with the gun still in his hand, he turned on his heel and went out into the hall. Laura heard the front door bang shut as she moved across to the bay window. She twitched the curtain aside. Kent's car was parked in the thin beam of a streetlamp. Laura saw him get in. The interior light was doused as the door closed.

She waited for the sounds of the engine starting, but they did not come. Instead she saw a little flare of orange from inside the car, followed by a sound like the bursting of an inflated paper bag.

THIRTY

Laura really liked Craig, the bulky youth who had helped Tom to save her life. So did Tom. In fact, Tom loved Craig.

'I'd known him for a while,' he explained to her later as they sat over lunch in her favourite Thai restaurant. 'I was really attracted, but I still held off.' He grinned wryly. 'Tried to be straight, conventional, live up to your nice middle-class standards, you see, "Mummy".'

'I haven't got nice middle-class standards,' Laura objected.

'Oh, but you have. They're the last things to die. Most inherited traits can be whittled away in a few generations, but if a family's ever been touched by the fatal kiss of the bourgeoisie, that never goes away.'

'Nonsense,' said Laura affectionately, delighted to see how much more relaxed her son had become.

'Emily was the last-ditch attempt on my part to be straight,' he went on. 'And for a time I thought it'd work. We got on well intellectually, I was quite happy to let her organize my life, I even began to think marriage was a possibility. You'd have been pleased if I'd got married, wouldn't you, "Mummy"?'

Laura just managed to curb her instinctive, 'not to Emily'. Mustn't speak ill of the dead, though she couldn't pretend that she'd found the girl anything other than a self-centred, repellent little prig.

'You see, with Emily it was only all right while it stayed platonic. Suited me well that she wanted to defer sex, you know, gave me more time to convince myself that the whole thing might work. But when we got into bed . . .' He shook his head ruefully. 'Can't pretend then, can you?'

'Did you actually hit her, though?'

'Yes. Yes, I suppose I did. The thing is . . . after an incredibly long preamble we finally made it to bed and . . . she started to touch me and . . . well, I knew absolutely then that that wasn't what I wanted. But she persisted, making advances, and I pushed her away . . . rather too forcibly, I guess. That's when she got the black eye.'

'Mm. And when you left me, you went straight to Craig's?'

Tom nodded, glowing with the memory. 'Straight to Craig's, and straight to bed. No doubts then. When sex is right, it all feels so incredibly natural, doesn't it?'

'Yes,' Laura agreed, a little wistfully. 'And, Tom, when you talked to me about not being able to change the nature you were born with, you were talking about your gayness?'

'Of course. What else did you think I was talking about?'

Laura gave a little shake of her head, indicating that it wasn't important. 'And that dossier, all that research you'd got under your bed . . .'

'Yes, that was my big project. You never talked about my father, where I came from. For some reason I didn't want to ask you directly, but I wanted to know. There was no way I wasn't going to be curious about it. And then I found out about my grandparents.'

'But why . . . with those photographs . . . why did you include the one of Emily?'

Tom shrugged. 'It was just the likeness. It seemed strange that all the women who were connected with my life looked so alike. I don't know, it was almost as if Emily had been singled out to meet me.'

'Singled out for a worse fate than that,' said Laura grimly.

Tom looked subdued and took a sip from his beer. 'That's still . . . I'm still finding it hard to come to terms with that. I mean, whatever I thought of Emily . . . she's the first, you know, of my generation . . . I mean, to think of someone of my age being dead, it's . . .'

Laura reached across and took her son's hand. With the other he wiped brusquely across his eyes. Time for the conversation to move on.

'What put you on to' . . . She couldn't bring herself to say 'your father' . . . 'the man who died in the police cell? Did you find that cutting I'd kept?'

He nodded.

'And did you know that he was your father?'

'I suspected it. I couldn't be sure. It spooked me sometimes, because the implication was definitely there that he'd killed Melanie Harris . . .'

'And you were worried that the evil might be hereditary?'

'What?' Tom looked at his mother in total puzzlement, then laughed. 'Good heavens, no. I don't believe in that sort of rubbish. The thought never occurred to me.'

So all Laura's care about keeping the truth of his origins from her son had been wasted. He had known the worst, and it hadn't worried him. If only they had been able to talk earlier. If only she had been honest and told him the truth.

'And what about Pauline Spanier, Tom? How on earth did you make the connection with her?'

'When you know nothing about your origins, you'll go to great lengths to find anything. I started reading papers from round the time of my conception. I found out about this strangling, and by then I was beginning to see some kind of pattern emerging.'

'Did you suspect Kent at that point?'

'No. It was all vague. I knew there was something there, but I couldn't make it all tie in.'

'Hm. Well, well done. I think you'll make a very good journalist, Tom.'

And Laura Fisher looked across at her son with pride. He was more separate from her now than ever. But he was his own person. A person with whom, in time, she might be able to form a relationship.

'Absolute fucking crap!'

'It's all very well for you to say that, Rob, but see it from my point of view. I've read books which would define me as the classic case. No strong male presence around while he was growing up — no male presence at all, really . . .'

'Except for little *moi*.'

'And you don't count.'

'Thank *you*. Charmed, I'm sure.'

'Anyway, then me as the dominant mother, preoccupied with my career . . . I mean, it could easily be that an upbringing like that would —'

' "My mother made me a homosexual"?'

'Yes.'

'That remark, Laura, is only good for one thing, which is as a feed for the graffiti which continues, "If I gave her the wool, would she make me one too?" Otherwise, it is, as I said, absolute fucking crap!'

'Well, you —'

'Listen, every gay I know — and I do know quite a few, dear — has known his sexual orientation virtually from birth. Some try to fight it, like Tom did, but deep down, we all know. It's nature, Laura, not fucking nurture.'

'Oh, well, if you say so.'

'I do say so.' A wistful look came into his faded eyes. 'And lucky Tom's got that hunk Craig. You know, I wouldn't mind a bit of that.'

'Don't think you stand a chance. Picture of domestic bliss, those two. Do you know, last weekend they were actually out choosing three-piece suites.'

Rob chuckled wheezily. Then suddenly he turned on Laura, his face pulled into an expression of injured martyrdom. 'Why didn't you bring me any fucking grapes, you mean cow?'

'Because you're getting better.'

'Don't you believe it. OK, this lot of chemotherapy seems to have staved it off for a little while. It'll be back.'

'May not be.'

'Huh. I'll put money on it. Not going to be much use to you as a partner, though, am I?'

'We'll see,' said Laura, though she had long since reconciled herself to the fact that she would always be running Lewthwaite Studios on her own. If Rob did come through, he was never going to be strong enough for the stresses an active partnership would involve.

'How are things going down at the coalface?' asked Rob.

'Oh, I survive,' said Laura.

And she did. Laura Fisher was a survivor.

Keeping the studios profitable got harder and harder. Television technology was changing so fast that the equipment she had originally fitted quickly became obsolete. To stand a chance against the opposition, she had to put herself further in debt and buy in the latest computerized editing machines.

But Laura Fisher was a worker, and she worked. The prospects for getting back into documentaries receded as she moved further away from the hub of the television business, but her training courses became more and more successful. With the income from those and the hire of facilities, Lewthwaite Studios slowly turned the corner into economic health.

Philip moved in with her soon after Kent's death, but three months later they split up. Three months after that, Philip, realizing the hopelessness of ever finishing his vaunted history of world broadcasting, went back to New Zealand. There, a year or two later, he married the mistress he had kept through Julie's long illness. He didn't love her, the sex was nothing near the magic he had shared with Laura, but she was familiar and she would look after him in his old age.

Laura Fisher missed Kent more than at times she could believe. A part of herself had died with him, and the sense of emptiness did not go away.

She never had another lover. She had been single too long to make room in her life for anyone else.